W9-DHV-764

Kacy

and

The Space Shuttle Secret

by Sharon Kahn

Illustrated by Mark Mitchell

EAKIN PRESS ★ Austin, Texas

Copyright © 1996
By Sharon Kahn

Published in the United States of America
By Eakin Press
An Imprint of Sunbelt Media, Inc.
P.O. Drawer 90159 ★ Austin, TX 78709-0159

ALL RIGHTS RESERVED. No part of this book may be repro-
duced in any form without written permission from the pub-
lisher, except for brief passages included in a review appearing in a newspaper or magazine.

ISBN 1-57168-025-X

3   4   5   6   7   8   9   10

Library of Congress Cataloging-in-Publication Data

Kahn, Sharon, 1934–
    Kacy and the space shuttle secret / by Sharon Kahn.
        p.   cm.
    Summary: Eleven-year-old Kacy Holiday's idea about sending a house-
plant on a shuttle mission into outer space has astronomical conse-
quences.
    ISBN 1-57168-025-X
    [1. Astronauts--Fiction. 2. Space shuttles--Fiction. 3. Kidnapping--
Fiction.] I. Title.
PZ7.K123434Kaj   1996
[Fic]--dc20
                                                                95-9740
                                                                    CIP
                                                                    AC

The story and characters within this book are fictional.

*This book is dedicated with love to my family —
always in my heart:
Suzy, David, Jon and Nancy,
and
especially to Emma and Camille.*

Contents

Space Shuttle Discovery
— Courtesy of NASA

Acknowledgments

Special thanks to NASA's Office of Public Information, Lyndon B. Johnson Space Center, Houston, Texas.

Thanks to all those who offered moral support, professional advice, and encouragement throughout this project: Ruthe Winegarten, Nancy R. Bell, Nancy L. Hendrickson, Daryl G. Fitzjerrell, Suzanne Bloomfield, Christina Neil, Lindsy Van Gelder, Ellen Vevier, Karen Casey Fitzjerrell, and the other members of The Shoal Creek Writers Group: Julie Rennecker, Dena Garcia, Eileen Joyce, and Gloria Amescua.

Edwin Eakin and Melissa Roberts supported the idea from its inception; Mark Mitchell brought it to life with his art.

The children who participated in the Bastrop Public Library's summer reading program were especially helpful with photograph selection.

Kacy knew she couldn't space out now. She had to think of a good answer so Mr. Wall would no longer loom above her . . .

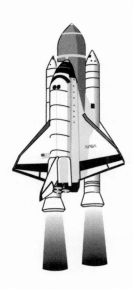

Chapter 1

Trouble in Dreamland

IN HER IMAGINATION, Kacy Holiday soared like a yellow butterfly over the deep green, rain-soaked woods behind her house. She was eleven years old, but secret mind-flying was something she had been doing for as long as she could remember. Her pale yellow butterfly wings were spread wide to pick up the faintest breezes wafting over Houston's treetops. As she floated on humid air currents, she leaned far to the right and dipped dangerously down toward the trees. She knew that balance had to be restored immediately in a downturn, but doing so was no easy trick. She used the central part of her butterfly body to stabilize her fall. By swinging carefully and quickly toward the left, but not so fast as to cause her see-through wings to shudder, Kacy rose with elegance from the turn.

Just as Kacy was preparing to whirl her body into a double spiral, sharp words shook the air around her.

"Kacy! Kacy Holiday! MISS Holiday!"

Kacy's head snapped to attention, but she was too

late. Her science teacher, Mr. Wall, was on the warpath. He was a large man, and though he was never pleased to have to wriggle through narrow aisles to reach her desk, he always considered it his duty to do so.

"Miss Holiday, do I now understand that the sixth grade once again has the pleasure of your company in this class? That you are with us in spirit as well as in body?" All the boys and Eileen Sorb snickered. Mr. Wall nodded to the snickerers and stroked his tiny black beard into a perfect triangle. "Just what is it that takes you away from us so often, Miss Holiday? Could you enlighten us?"

Kacy knew she couldn't space out now. She had to think of a good answer so Mr. Wall would no longer loom above her, blocking her view of the best window in class. Her hand slipped around to the back of her neck, her fingers beginning to twirl her red ponytail — a sure sign she needed comfort. She twisted her long, thin body into a snail's shape while she thought. Coiling up might help her decide, pronto, which category of trouble she was into. If Mr. Wall were just mildly mad, she might be able to joke her way out of this. But if it were one of those last straw situations, he might only accept complete surrender. She decided on complete surrender. After all, Mr. Wall had visited her aisle twice this week already. Kacy knew kids who pushed things to the limit every time, and she was not one of them. She saved her battles for the really important moments.

"I'm sorry, Mr. Wall. Could you repeat the question?" She assumed there *was* a question, or at least she hoped so.

Mr. Wall did what she knew he would do — he leaned on her desk while he was talking. She hated that. His tweed jacket with the leather elbows brushed across all her papers, messing them up. She told herself not to think about it for now. She had to use her concentration to deal with an all too familiar scene: her science teacher using her as an example for the rest of the class, and the rest of the class enjoying her misery. Well, not *everybody*. She knew her friends were silently groaning for her — Sonya and Bethany, for sure.

Mr. Wall was in no mood to let up. "Yes, there is a question for you, Miss Holiday. Are you planning to take part in the Science Fair with the rest of us? So far, you have rejected every idea I've proposed to you. Martin Goodfellow was willing to work with you on categories of minerals found in abundance in the Houston area, but he reported to me that he never heard from you concerning that plan. The project is very appropriate to this grade level — unlike some of your more unusual suggestions, I might add."

Kacy groaned. Martin Goodfellow was the last person she wanted to team up with. He was Mr. Wall's pet pupil, and he had a habit of peering at Kacy over his glasses as though she were a bug in a jar. She put her head on her desk, carefully avoiding the part of the desk being leaned on by Mr. Wall. Eileen Sorb giggled. Kacy's head hurt. School made her so tired lately. She wished she could just go live by the Gulf in Galveston and read all the time — whenever she wasn't running on the beach. She peeked beneath her arm and saw that Mr. Wall was still there and showed no signs of leaving. In fact, he was just warming up.

"You don't still have that ridiculous idea in your head to be a child astronaut?"

"No, sir." At times like this Kacy felt like giving up and never explaining anything again. A *child astronaut*? What a dumb way to put it. She had never said she wanted to be a *child astronaut*. They'd never take someone her age. What she wanted was much simpler. She wanted to prepare a science project to be taken on board a space flight, and in her dreams, she saw herself handing it over to one of the cool women who, as astronauts, trained only a few miles from her school. Didn't anyone in this class realize how lucky they were to be living in Houston, right in the heart of the space program? Just thinking about it gave her the courage for one more try.

3

"Mr. Wall, I just want to do a space shuttle project for NASA." Mr. Wall always made them call NASA by its full name, the National Aeronautics and Space Administration, but Kacy tried to ignore that. "I have this idea for growing plants. It's very simple — not too advanced for sixth grade. It's even more exciting than working with seeds grown in space. I'll pick a plant and make all kinds of observations about it before it goes up in a space shuttle, and then I'll monitor what happens to it after it gets back."

Mr. Wall shook his head. "And the astronauts chosen by our country to make an important mission will have nothing better to do than water your plant?"

"I figure I'll never know if I don't ask them. Or ask somebody. We had an astronaut come to the school once, and he seemed really neat. He said we could ask him anything."

Mr. Wall had a smirk on his face and the class laughed as if she were the dumbest person they'd ever met. Maybe she was. Maybe it *was* dumb to have dreams and then try to believe they might come true. Even her mom had taken a long time to get used to what she called "Kacy's flying thing."

Kacy's mother worked as a bookkeeper for the biggest Chevy agency in Houston. You might think she knew a lot about cars, but she didn't. Not about their insides, anyway. She told Kacy she knew about the important things, though, like how to pay for them. That didn't seem as interesting to Kacy as figuring out what made them work. Kacy bet her dad would have known about cars *and* planes. He had been a petroleum engineer, working in the big oil fields near Odessa. Kacy was sure he'd flown in all sorts of planes. He died falling from an oil rig when she was two, so she'd never been able to find out from him all the neat stuff he did in his work. She used to ask her mom all the time, but her mom just got tired when Kacy tried to talk about it.

Kacy's big brother, Tom, had been only seven when

4

their dad died, so he didn't have a real good memory of Dad's work — not good enough to satisfy Kacy. He did seem to understand her fascination with planes and space shuttles, though, and he explained it to their mom as something like his own love for cars. Mom had found a job for him, washing cars at the Chevy dealership. Lucky him. He got to wash down the new cars just after they arrived dirty from traveling on the big trailer trucks from Michigan and Ohio. If it weren't for Tom, those cars would never look brand new and beautiful. He got to open the hoods and look at the clean engines, too, before they got all gooky from use.

Thank goodness for Tom. He was Kacy's best friend at home. He liked her even though he was already sixteen and in high school. He even liked her green eyes, which everyone else thought were weird because they weren't blue or brown like most people's. He also reminded her that her eyesight was 20-20 at her checkup, and that the eye doctor had told her she had jet pilot eyes — a wide field of vision. That made her happy.

Kacy wished she were on the playground where people didn't talk much. Nobody laughed at her there, especially when she hit those long balls on the softball field. She felt all stretched out when she was on the playground. School was easier to take when she wasn't cramped up indoors. Her long legs made her a good runner, and she could outrun most of the boys. Her P.E. teacher had told her she was very coordinated.

Mr. Wall shifted his arms on her desk, and Kacy was sure he was finally going to leave her alone. Instead, he lifted her science workbook from the desktop and peered under it. Kacy felt her face flushing as he brought out a *Best Computer* magazine she had borrowed from her brother.

"And what is this?" he asked, holding the magazine by its edge as if it would dirty his fingers.

"It has an article about computers in Beechcraft cockpits." Kacy's headache seemed to have been replaced by a pain in her stomach. With her luck, Mr. Wall wouldn't have even heard of a Beechcraft small plane.

She never got to find out whether Mr. Wall knew about Beechcrafts. "What's this magazine doing in science class?" he rephrased his question. "Do you remember what I told you I would do next time I found a magazine or book under your workbook?"

"Yes, sir."

"And what is that?"

Kacy could feel the rest of the class waiting for the ax to fall. "Send me to the counselor's office?"

"Congratulations, Miss Holiday. You have finally remembered something I've told you. Your inattention in this class has reached the limit of my patience." Mr. Wall dropped *Best Computer* on her desk, where it slid down under her feet. Kacy dove under the desk to get it. She stayed under for a minute, trying to avoid what she knew was about to come.

"Get up, Kacy," her friend Sonya whispered from the next desk. "It's hopeless."

Kacy refused to believe it was totally hopeless. She came up from under her desk with her hand raised, and didn't wait for Mr. Wall to call on her. She had noticed that he didn't call on girls all that much anyway, even if their hands were raised. "Mr. Wall, could I ask you something privately?" He was back at his desk, and she walked quickly up to him, not looking at the desks on either side of her.

"Would you consider a deal?" Kacy tried a loud whisper, though she had never been particularly good at that.

"A deal?" he boomed.

It was too late to care if everyone heard. Kacy forged ahead. "Yes, sir. If I can get NASA interested in my science project, would you let me do it then? And maybe the counselor thing could wait?"

"The National Aeronautics and Space Administration *interested*?" Mr. Wall laughed. "Miss Holiday, your imagination knows no bounds. On the day America's

6

Space Administration takes your science project into space, I'll shave my beard." The class laughed, and Mr. Wall took a little bow. "Martin Goodfellow, you are a hall monitor, are you not?" Mr. Wall looked at Martin, who nodded. "Then would you do me the favor to escort Miss Holiday to Counselor Harris' office?"

Kacy gave up. There was nothing she could do now but follow Martin Goody-Goody down the hall. Ms. Harris would not be happy to see her for the second time in a month, and her mother would not be happy to receive the note which followed these visits.

Martin didn't just walk down the hall — he marched like a little soldier. He was shorter than she was and marched in little steps, so she had to walk really slowly to stay behind him. She wanted to take her time. If there were half a hallway between them, maybe no one would think they were together.

Kacy wondered why her stomach had stopped hurting, especially with such an ordeal ahead of her. For a few seconds she couldn't figure it out, but suddenly she knew. Her teacher may have been making fun of her, but something else had just happened in the classroom. Whether he realized it or not, Mr. Wall had just made a deal.

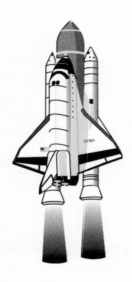

Chapter 2

Kacy Writes to an Astronaut

KACY WAS TREMBLING just a little bit as she glimpsed Ms. Harris' familiar doorway with the river-rafting poster taped to it. That was cool, she thought. She wished she were canoeing over the rapids right now instead of heading toward punishment row.

"You can go now, Martin," Kacy said, annoyed that he was still hanging around to witness the worst.

"Don't you think Ms. Harris ought to dismiss me?" He was his usual smug self, and he planted his stocky corduroy pant-legs in front of the door until Kacy gave him one of her looks and he took off. One less thing to worry about.

She tapped on Ms. Harris' door and heard a cheery "Come in." Ms. Harris could afford to be cheery, of course; she was the grown-up. Still, it was better to be facing her than somebody worse. As Kacy opened the door, Martin, the sneak, dashed around the corner where he must have been hiding and pushed in front of her.

"Ms. Harris, I've been sent by Mr. Wall to report that

Kacy has been caught reading magazines under her science textbook again. Do you want me to stay in case you have any reply?"

"No, Martin. It's not likely I'd have a reply before Kacy and I have talked," Ms. Harris said. "You can go now. Thank you."

Martin finally left the room with a stupid glance at Kacy. This was so humiliating. Kacy started to say that Mr. Wall hadn't asked Martin to report to her, but she was so angry she couldn't get it all together. She just looked at Ms. Harris. "This is what I have to put up with," was all she could say.

To Kacy's surprise, Ms. Harris' lips turned up in what looked like a smile. A very small turn-up, but it was definitely in the smile category.

"One of those days, huh, Kacy? Why don't you sit down? Want a drink of water?"

"No, thank you." Kacy felt her cheeks. They were still hot. Why do redheads blush so much? The whole world knows your feelings if you're a redhead.

Ms. Harris' skirts and blouses didn't look like the other teachers'. She dressed in soft, full skirts with patterned borders around the hemline, and blouses with scooped necklines. She was African-American, with honey-colored skin. Kacy imagined Ms. Harris could have been a Mayan princess. She obviously didn't have to worry about blushing every time she turned around, either.

So much for the smile; she was dead serious now. Kacy wondered what the best approach would be. She hemmed and hawed for a couple of minutes, then broke down and told Ms. Harris all about her idea for the science project, Mr. Wall's visit to her desk, and how all the kids laughed at her.

"Funny, but you forgot to mention the reason Mr. Wall sent you to my office," Ms. Harris said. "It's amazing how often people forget those things."

"I'd finished all my reading," Kacy told her. "Why

would he care about an old magazine, anyhow? It was just *Best Computers*. That's science too. It's not even a magazine I like that much. I'd read everything else in the house and I found it in the bathroom."

The smile almost made an appearance again, but at the last minute, Ms. Harris tightened up her face. "This thing between you and Mr. Wall, Kacy — don't you think it's gone far enough? I'd call it a power struggle, wouldn't you? And you're too smart not to know where the power is in that classroom."

Kacy relaxed a little and let out a big sigh. It wasn't a lot of fun trying to get around Ms. Harris, because she always took the wind out of your sails. At least she didn't try to paint everything as good or bad like Mr. Wall did. But there was still work to be done here and Kacy decided she'd better not get too distracted.

"Are you going to write a note to my mom?" Kacy was actually afraid Ms. Harris would ask her mom to come to school, so maybe this note idea would ward her off. "My mom's been working a lot of overtime lately, and she's really tired when she gets home. I wouldn't want to overload her."

"No, we certainly wouldn't want to do that, would we? So why don't you shape up so we can avoid that?"

Kacy thought she saw a ray of light. "I promise that next time . . ."

"It's too late for that, Kacy. I can't go back to Mr. Wall and tell him I've done nothing about this. I'm writing your mom a note and you'll have to take what comes from that. But I'm also concerned about your progress in that class. If I remember, you've received straight C's."

"That's because he counts off for bad behavior. I really do want to make up for that with my project, but he won't listen."

"You're really serious about wanting to do this, aren't you?" Ms. Harris looked hard at her.

"It's the first thing all year I haven't been bored with," Kacy admitted, although she knew from bitter experience that these school people thought the word "bored" meant "cocky," and this was no time to make Ms. Harris mad. She seemed to be taking it OK, though.

"You know, Kacy, I've been thinking. Maybe you should do some more detailed research on this project before you present it to Mr. Wall. It does seem farfetched, and maybe he needs to see that you've given it some concrete thought before he lets you go ahead. Let's make our own agreement. I'll help you make some plans, and if they work out, I promise I'll put in a good word for you with your teacher."

"Do you mean it? I have a zillion plans!"

"What's the first thing you want to do?" Ms. Harris got out her notepad.

"I want to get in touch with a woman astronaut. Do you know any?"

"No, but NASA has a Public Information Office. Would you like to call them?" She pointed to the phone on her desk.

"Right now?"

"Do you want to do it later at home?"

Kacy thought of the atmosphere that was likely to prevail at her house that night and decided to make her call now. Besides, it would give her something to tell her mom after the firestorm. This was also getting her out of the rest of science class, and she couldn't bear the thought of facing Mr. Wall *and* her mom in the same day.

The Public Information Office was very helpful. A worker there gave Kacy the names of several female astronauts and suggested she write to one or all of them. Kacy decided to write one at a time and see what happened.

Ms. Harris said Kacy had done very well on the phone, and suggested she compose a letter to one of the women, and she would add a cover note to it. Kacy liked the name Rosa Ruiz.

"It sounds more friendly than the others, don't you think?"

11

Ms. Harris laughed. "I'm not quite sure what's in a name that could give you that idea, but why not? Go for it."

Kacy borrowed Ms. Harris' yellow lined pad, put it in her lap, and began to print. She felt her printing was better than her writing, and looked more official:

DEAR ROSA RUIZ,

MY NAME IS KACY HOLIDAY AND I AM A SIXTH GRADER AT KENNEDY SCHOOL. I NEED YOUR HELP RIGHT AWAY, IF THAT'S NOT TOO MUCH TROUBLE. YOU SEE, I AM SUPPOSED TO HAVE A PROJECT FOR OUR SPRING SCIENCE FAIR, AND MY IDEA IS TO SEND A VERY SMALL PLANT INTO SPACE ON ONE OF NASA'S SPACE SHUTTLES. TAKE MY WORD FOR IT THAT IT WILL TAKE UP ONLY THE TEENIEST AMOUNT OF SPACE.

I WILL TAKE SOME TESTS AND MEASUREMENTS BEFORE AND AFTER, TO SEE IF IT HAS GROWN OR CHANGED OR EVEN (I HOPE NOT) DIED. MY TEACHER SAYS YOU WILL NOT HAVE TIME TO WATER IT, BUT I'D LIKE TO ASK YOU MYSELF, JUST TO MAKE SURE. I FIGURE I WON'T KNOW IF I DON'T TRY. I'M ALSO WONDERING JUST HOW YOU WILL BE ABLE TO WATER IT IF WEIGHTLESSNESS IN SPACE SENDS THE WATER UPWARDS. I HAVE SOME IDEAS ABOUT THAT.

I WOULD LIKE VERY MUCH TO MEET YOU IN PERSON AND GIVE YOU MY PLANT, BUT I KNOW YOU ARE BUSY AND MAYBE I'LL HAVE TO SEND IT TO YOU. THIS ISN'T A VERY GOOD IDEA NOW THAT I THINK OF IT, BECAUSE WHO KNOWS WHAT SHAPE IT WILL BE IN WHEN IT GETS THERE? AS YOU CAN SEE, I NEED LOTS OF ADVICE. PLEASE WRITE ME RIGHT AWAY OR AS SOON AS POSSIBLE.

YOUR FRIEND,
KACY

"The letter is great, Kacy." Ms. Harris took a school envelope, put Kacy's name on it in care of her office, and handed it back to her. Kacy wrote "URGENT" all over it with a red marker.

"I think it should go Priority Mail," she told Ms. Harris.

"That takes ten stamps," Ms. Harris told her.

"I only have five stamps at home."

"I'll go halves with you, and put five of my own on when I add the cover note," Ms. Harris said. "Or . . . let's send it today, and you can bring me the stamps tomorrow."

Ms. Harris really *was* an amazing woman. Kacy was so excited it almost made up for the fact that she had to go home and face the music.

"Let's keep this to ourselves for a few days," Ms. Harris advised. "What do you think?"

"I think it's a good idea," Kacy said, "but I'd like to tell my brother and my mom." Maybe her mom wouldn't be so mad at her if she knew Ms. Harris wasn't.

"Kacy Holiday, you have your wheels turning all the time," Ms. Harris told her as she shook her hand in a businesslike manner.

"Well, thanks," Kacy said as she started out the door.

"Forget something?" Ms. Harris handed her a sealed envelope addressed to her mom. Kacy groaned. When had she had time to write that with all the more important stuff that went on this afternoon?

They both managed a smile before she left. But if either one of them had known at that moment what unbelievable adventures were in store for Kacy and her tiny plant, their palms might have been sweaty, at the very least.

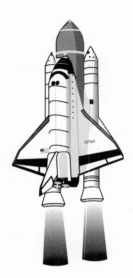

Chapter 3

Grounded

KACY DIDN'T EXACTLY start racing home. She stopped to get a slushy at the corner 7-11. The root beer flavor usually calmed her down, but it didn't help all that much this afternoon. When she reached the halfway mark in her ten-block walk home — the big live oak — she realized she shouldn't be dawdling. She had plenty to do before Mom got home, so she ran the rest of the way to her house and jumped the two steps to the front porch. The porch swing looked like a tempting place to finish her drink, but she sacrificed. She felt a little too guilty to reward herself.

She put the big silver key in the lock, tightened her stomach like she always did when she opened the door into the silent house, and did her quick look-around to make sure nobody was behind the furniture. Kacy never told Mom or Tom about this ritual. She was sure it would have seemed wimpy to them. Even though she knew she could always handle things, and no one ever *had* been behind the furniture, it was still the teeniest bit scary. Maybe a *lot* scary on dark, rainy days.

Kacy made a quick leap for the sofa, landing easily on her back and getting into phone-call mode. She slid a sofa pillow under her head and dialed Sonya. Nuts. A busy signal. If Sonya were on the phone with Bethany, she'd have to wait for both of them. Then again, Bethany had call waiting, so she could easily find out. Bethany answered.

"Are you on the phone?" Kacy asked.

"Nope. What happened in the counselor's office? You never came back to class."

"That's because the bell rang and I got to miss the last part of science. Well, there's good news and bad news. The bad news is I have a note for mom. The good news is I got to write a letter to an astronaut."

Bethany's opinion was that Kacy had gotten off easy, especially seeing how mad Mr. Wall had been. On the other hand, she was unhappy that Kacy would probably be grounded, since they'd planned to see a movie Friday night.

"Do you think your mom would consider letting me rent a video and bring it over?"

"I doubt it, Bethy. But we have more important things to discuss, and I don't have much time. How do you think I should approach this?"

Bethany laughed. Kacy could picture her friend laughing. Unlike tiny, blond Sonya, Bethany was a big-boned girl, twice as thick as Kacy was, and she laughed with her whole body. Kacy imagined Bethany's thick black braid of hair shaking.

"Approach? Why are you worried about approaches all of a sudden?" Bethany asked. "You've certainly had more practice at this than Sonya and I have."

"I can't help it if you're tamer, Bethy. Besides, you've got to admit, I'm always the one they look for and always the one they catch. You're luckier."

"Yeah, right. Luckier. Try smarter."

Kacy knew she had a point. Her two friends didn't throw themselves into things without thinking. She did, and quite often. But she loved the easy way her friends understood her. If everybody were like this, she thought, she'd be a lot better off.

"Back to the point," Kacy said. "Do you think I ought to come right out with it and *suggest* a punishment? Maybe she'd appreciate the honesty."

"What are you having for dinner?"

"Huh? Thanks for answering my question. Mom's bringing home chicken from Country Bob's."

"Well, since it's something good, I think you ought to wait until after dinner so you won't be sent away from the table, then give her the note while she's still in a good mood from the barbecue. And I wouldn't suggest anything."

Kacy heard the screen door banging. "Bethy, I think I hear Tom, and I don't have much time. Thanks for the advice. Can I call you back?"

"Sure. Let me know what he says. Want me to call Sonya and tell her?"

"Yeah. Bye." Kacy jumped up to give Tom a hug. She banged her face against his big goggles. Tom rode the same bike he'd had for years now, but he liked to wear motorcycle goggles. Kacy suspected he did a fair amount of imagining, too, but he didn't talk about it.

"OK, what's up, Squirt? What's the hug for?" Tom had called her Squirt from way back, even though now she was a couple of inches taller than most girls her age. And he never let her get away with anything.

"Can't I even hug my own brother?"

"Quit the bull, Kace." *Kace* was better. One thing she liked about Tom was that although he usually got in one big brother jab, he was never a boring jerk about it like Sonya's brother, who would stupidly repeat something until it was coming out of your ears. Most of the time, Tom called her by her regular name, or a short version of it.

"OK, Bro. You got me with the hug. This is today's

16

worry . . ." Kacy repeated her story for the second time, with only her mom to go. Bethany would tell Sonya, no doubt about that, so she wouldn't have to recite this a fourth time.

Tom chewed on the inside of his cheek like he usually did when he was concentrating, and Kacy knew not to interrupt him. He was a good thinker, and she could certainly use that.

"I'd say it's a three-dayer," he said. "Bottom line, three days grounding. Could have been more without Harris giving you a break. Why beat around the bush with Mom? Just tell her, straight out."

Bethany's idea about waiting until after the barbecue chicken was a good one. Nothing special happened at dinner except for Tom leaning over and whispering to her that the prospect of punishment didn't seem to have affected her appetite. It hadn't, mostly because she was so excited about the letter she had written. Trouble was, she couldn't very well tell her mom about that without talking about the visit to Ms. Harris' office, so she just had to bide her time. She loved chicken wings and nobody else in the family cared about them, so she spent her time at dinner concentrating on those and the red beans and rice, a specialty of Country Bob's. Tom had to get on her case, as usual, for poking through her beans.

"Why do you pick through your food like that?" he asked. "You pull apart bread in a peanut butter sandwich, you fork through spaghetti — are you looking for gold or something?" Mom, of course, told her it was bad manners.

Kacy tried to explain once again. "I'm sorry. I can't mix foods on my plate and I absolutely have to know what's in the stuff I eat. Maybe I can learn to pick through it so no one sees me."

Mom looked really tired. Tom and Kacy hated to see her come home so exhausted. It was worse these days,

17

because she was having to do the bookkeeping work of two people. The other bookkeeper the car agency had hired was a total goof-off, and he got fired. They never hired a replacement, and the extra work was loaded on Mom.

Kacy thought her mom was pretty for an older woman. She had auburn hair, several shades darker than Kacy's, and it was cut in a short, cute style. It was one of the things she splurged on, she said. She was slender, and unlike Kacy and Tom, never ate much. She said she ate all the wrong things at work, out of nervousness, and wasn't hungry when she should be. She wanted her kids to eat healthier. They did, most of the time. Kacy was scared of what Mom called her *ultimatums*, but she really liked the way she didn't try to hold herself up to her kids as some sort of perfect being. Not that she was all that great when her kids had done something a little risky that backfired — especially when she was tired, like tonight.

"I'll clear the table and rinse the dishes. You can put them in the dishwasher when I'm finished," Kacy told Tom. *Uh-oh . . . I should have never volunteered like that — Mom and Tom know I have to be asked to do the dishes.* Tom rolled his eyes toward the top of his head, and Kacy winced. It had been a dumb move. Putting the dishes in the dishwasher was nothing, especially after the grease was rinsed off them. Tom, as usual, was right. Mom was onto her immediately.

"I *thought* you were too quiet tonight. I don't want to deal with this," Mom said as she brushed her hair back with her hands. "The end of a perfect day."

"Gee, Mom, you don't even know what it is yet." Kacy was feeling put upon already, but she looked at Tom's face and decided she'd better shut up.

"You can leave now, Tom," her mom said.

This was getting serious. Kacy felt so much better when Tom stayed. Not that he was able to do much when Mom was tired *and* mad.

Mom looked at her. "Spill it." She meant business.

Kacy took Ms. Harris' folded note out of her jeans pocket and handed it over.

"It's not as bad as it seems, Mom. There's a whole other thing that happened . . ."

Mom didn't hear her. She had taken the note and her coffee and was headed into the living room.

"I feel like smoking a cigarette," she said.

"Mom! You said you only smoked for one year, after Dad died. You wouldn't . . ."

"No, I wouldn't, Kacy. That's what I *feel* like doing. It's not what I'm going to do. There's a difference. Just let me read this, will you?"

"I'm sure this won't go on my permanent record, Mom."

Mom looked older while she was reading the note. Her face seemed to sag a bit.

"Why can't you get along, Kacy? You're smart enough to know people are different. Why would it be *your* luck to have an entire schedule of wonderful teachers when no one else would expect to hit the jackpot one hundred percent of the time? Maybe you don't like him, but so what? Why can't you just deal with it? Why pick him to aggravate?"

She was off and running. Kacy knew she'd just have to wait until it was over. Part of her understood what her mom meant. Mom was one of those people who just weathered things and got along. But surely she'd never endured a Mr. Wall type. How could Kacy just sit there when he made her feel so foolish in front of the class? He just didn't think she was worth anything — that's the part she couldn't stand. Reading those magazines under cover was the only way she could keep her sanity in there, and now, even that wasn't working. Where was Tom when she needed him?

"Kacy, what will you be doing when you're fourteen and fifteen? That's what I'm worried about. If you're in the counselor's office all the time at eleven, it's only going to get worse as you get older."

19

"I'm sorry, Mom. And don't you dare smoke. I'm not worth *that*. What would we do if you got lung cancer and died?" Kacy forgot about the situation she was in and ran over to fling her arms around her mom.

They both cried. "Honey, I'm just so tired," Mom said. "At least I won't have to go to school this time. But Ms. Harris is as frustrated as I am. She knows you could make better grades if you just didn't push the limits. Why do you do it?"

"I don't know, Mom. What are you going to do?"

"I don't want you going out for the rest of this week, including the weekend."

"The weekend? Tom thought this was only a three-day thing at the least."

Kacy realized *that* was the wrong thing to say, but it was already out of her mouth. Tom was right. This was her problem — she never knew when to quit.

"Mr. Tom knows all the answers, doesn't he?" Mom said. "He can see right into my mind and predict what I'm going to do and say. Maybe he can have a career as a fortune-teller."

The weekend. Bummer. And if Tom were listening, he'd make her life miserable as well. She heard the back door screen slam as he left to go hang out with his friends. He'd heard. Now it was just Kacy and Mom for the evening.

"The rest of the day was good, Mom. Wanna hear?"

"No. Go do your homework. No phone tonight, either."

Kacy went upstairs to her room and closed the door. She flopped on the bedspread, being careful not to land with a bang that might shake the floor. That's all she would need. No calling Sonya, even. Sonya would have to rely on what Bethany told her, and everyone knew Bethany never got anything straight the first time.

What a day. She wanted to mope for a while, and she definitely felt like crying about this grounding, but she

20

made herself pull out her math homework. No use getting in more trouble. Math always went the fastest. It was easy tonight. She didn't even know what was assigned in science for tomorrow. This could be a reason to call one of her friends later, if Mom relented. Thinking about Rosa Ruiz might turn things around, too, but she saved that for later. At least she could go to sleep feeling good about the astronaut letter.

Fortunately, after she did her math she remembered to kick off her sneakers because of the new bedspread. They were pretty nasty. She had them off by the time Mom came upstairs and knocked on her door.

"How's the homework coming?"

"Fine." Kacy knew she had a choice here. She could sulk and not say much to Mom, or she could open up and see if the storm was over. She was dying to tell about her NASA plan, so she decided not to sulk. "Mom, can I tell you what else happened today?"

"That's what I came up to hear," Mom said, and flopped on the bed too.

Kacy told her all about the plans made with Ms. Harris, the urgent letter to Rosa Ruiz, and the chance that her plant might go up in space. It wasn't the greatest chance, but it *was* a chance.

Mom seemed really happy about it all. Her face looked so much better than it had at the dinner table. Her eyes were really pretty when she was happy.

"I'm thrilled, honey. Ms. Harris is really a peach, isn't she? I hope it all works out for you."

Mom was in such a good mood, she even let Kacy make a quick call to Bethany, but only to get her homework. She stuck around while Kacy made the call. Afterwards, Kacy figured it wouldn't hurt to see if Mom *really* meant to separate her from the whole world for an entire week.

"So, how about it, Mom? Could you skip the weekend

part of the grounding — maybe in celebration of my meeting the astronaut?"

"Sorry, babe," Mom said as she breezed out the door of Kacy's room. "You know I never go back on my word."

Kacy flopped back on her bed, muttering to herself. "Just wait. I'll show all of you."

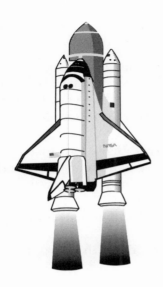

Chapter 4

An Important Phone Call

BY THE FOURTH DAY of grounding, Kacy was going nuts. It was so boring coming straight home after school, but she figured if she had made it through the weekend, she could do anything. She read, did chores, washed her hair, and daydreamed all weekend. She tried TV, too, but turned it off after a few minutes.

Monday morning she took off for school early. Anything was better than hanging around the house — even school. If the opening bell hadn't rung yet, she could always ask one of the teachers if she could go to the library. Not that she hadn't read everything good in there already.

Kacy had her own private hopscotch ritual for going up the school steps: one hop up for each consonant in the name of her favorite movie star, and one hop down for each vowel. As she headed for the door, she almost ran into Ms. Harris, who was coming in from the parking lot, loaded down with papers and files.

"How about a hand with these, Kacy?"

"Sure, give me all the heavy ones. I'm very strong. I can carry more than my brother can. I'll take all of them."

"Part will be fine. We'll each take an armful."

Ms. Harris unlocked her office door and pointed Kacy toward one of the tables inside. Just as she was dumping the books, the phone rang in Ms. Harris' inner office.

"Hello?"

Kacy waited while Ms. Harris answered, just to be polite and not run off. Also because of her curious streak.

"Why, yes, this is an excellent place to contact her. In fact, she happens to be here right now."

Kacy's ears perked up and a shiver ran down the back of her neck.

"It's Rosa Ruiz," Ms. Harris said with a big grin on her face.

Kacy could hardly believe it. She felt a little shy about taking the phone. She'd never talked to an astronaut before.

"What do I say to her?" she whispered.

"Why don't you wait to see what she has to say?" Ms. Harris handed her the phone with no help at all, so there was nothing to do but take a breath and face it.

"Kacy," Rosa said, "I received your urgent letter and decided to phone instead of writing back. You don't have much time to make a decision about your science project, do you?"

"No, ma'am. Mr. Wall, my teacher, says I'm late already, and he's going to take off points before I even get started if I don't decide in a hurry."

Rosa's voice sounded really nice. Kacy had already, in her daydreams, put the two of them on a first-name basis, but she remembered to call her "Ms. Ruiz" over the phone. She wished she could meet her. She pictured Rosa as having brown hair to her shoulders and green eyes. Tom said she was always jumping to conclusions about people, but she didn't care. It was fun.

"I do want to help you out, Kacy, especially since we're both in the Houston area. I'm currently training for a flight on the space shuttle *Discovery,* and before long, we'll be going down to the launch site in Florida. Because

I'm so busy, I have only a few speaking engagements scheduled, but I've had a cancellation for a school talk next week. Would you like to have me come to your class?"

"You? Come to my class?" Kacy couldn't contain herself — she had to jump up and down. "She's coming here! Here!" she yelled to Ms. Harris. Then turning her mouth back to the phone, "This is so wonderful, I — I —"

"Why don't you let me talk to Ms. Harris — the teacher who added a cover note to your letter — and maybe we can make some arrangements."

"That's my school counselor. She's right here." Kacy had to admit she was relieved to hand over the phone. She'd been so excited she didn't know what else to say, and Ms. Harris never seemed to have that problem. Kacy's palms were sweating so, the phone almost slipped out of her hand when she tried to pass it over. She couldn't wait to learn what kind of arrangements Rosa was planning.

Just then the bell rang for homeroom, and Ms. Harris waved her off, covering the mouthpiece on the phone.

"Don't you think I should stay?"

"I promise to tell you everything she says. I don't want you late for homeroom — you don't need any more trouble."

"I really think I need to be here — "

"Don't blow it, Kacy." Ms. Harris gave her one of those looks she knew it was hopeless to fight. Her mother's look. "Don't call me — I'll call you." She smiled. "I'll find you as soon as I can. Just hold on. And if I were you, I'd keep this to myself until all the plans are made."

Kacy raced to homeroom, to her seat in the next to the last row, between Bethany and Sonya.

"You won't believe what just happened," she whispered between breaths.

She told them all about her news during roll call. She figured telling her two closest friends *was* just like keeping it to herself.

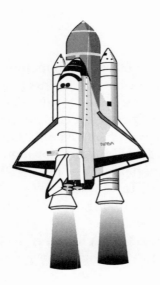

Chapter 5

Rosie Comes to Class

THE DAY HAD arrived. All eyes were on Rosa Ruiz as she bounded into Mr. Wall's classroom. A "Wow" came from the back of the room as the tall astronaut, wearing a bright blue NASA-emblazoned flight suit and burnished dark wine-colored boots, walked to the front of the classroom and shook Mr. Wall's hand. She had a firm handshake. In fact, everything about her looked strong and lean.

Rosa took off her sunglasses, put them in the zippered pocket slanting to one side of her coverall, and turned to grin widely at the awestruck science class. She asked the class to call her by her nickname, Rosie. The school principal, Mr. Traynor, accompanied Rosie, along with Ms. Harris. They both looked very pleased.

Mr. Wall gave Rosie a big smile, and Kacy wondered what Rosie would have thought if she'd seen his face a few days ago, when she and Ms. Harris had surprised him with the news that an astronaut wanted to visit. He had sputtered, not seeming all that pleased until Ms.

Harris reminded him what an honor this was, and how Rosie had preferred to speak only to his class rather than to the whole school. Kacy was sure his hesitation had been because the visit was her idea.

"Do you mean this woman is really interested in a schoolgirl's plant?" he had questioned when Kacy and Ms. Harris met with him in the counselor's office after school.

Ms. Harris had made sure he understood. "Astronaut Ruiz feels that this project will make science students like Kacy feel more a part of the government's space efforts. We were lucky to have reached her at the right time with the right project. I'm sure there will be some favorable publicity for the school science program too."

Ms. Harris always was very persuasive. By the time Mr. Wall told the class and saw their excited response, he was in high spirits. And by the day of the visit, his classroom was covered with welcome posters and student artwork. This was a big occasion.

On the big day, Mr. Wall was wearing a bright yellow flowered tie. Kacy had talked her mom into letting her wear her new vest — a very excellent green and gold paisley print.

Rosie Ruiz stood before the class and thanked Mr. Wall for allowing her to visit. He thanked her for coming and told her that Kacy was one of his ". . . uh . . . most interesting students." Rosie received this information with a nod, but the class laughed — knowing just how interesting Mr. Wall thought she was.

"Kacy Holiday has asked if we can carry a plant into space and monitor any changes that occur during orbit. I've talked to the scientists planning the projects and have received permission to include Kacy's experiment. When we return from our flight, Kacy can help us compare that plant with one she will keep here on Earth. She can then write up her project for Mr. Wall as part of her science assignment. Do you have any questions about the project or about my work?"

The class had many questions. Bethany wanted to

know how Rosie was selected for the astronaut program. She learned that it had been a long and well-planned process.

"I was selected as a mission specialist," Rosie told the class. "The mission specialist astronauts work with the commander and pilot and coordinate many shuttle operations. We plan crew activity and meals and are responsible for the experiments done on board. We perform extravehicular activities too. Perhaps you've seen us controlling the robot shuttle arms that reach out in space."

Bethany, not finished asking her question, kept going. "But how did you get to be an astronaut?"

"First I discovered how much fun science and math could be. I studied chemistry and biology in college and made good grades — A's and B-pluses. I went on to get a doctoral degree in the biological sciences, and worked for a government program in biomedical research. I'm very interested in studies of the blood cells. One of the things we're studying is what happens to a person's blood cells when that person has been in space for many days."

Rosie told how scared she was when she went for a whole week of interviews at NASA, and how her friends threw a big party for her when she was selected for astronaut training at the Houston facility. After the party came all the hard work. "We learned an awful lot about computers, " she said. "We couldn't be up and running in space without them. And we learn every detail of our spacecraft."

Martin Goodfellow raised his hand. "I know all about waste elimination in space," he announced.

"What's that?" Eileen Sorb asked.

"Are you talking about how we astronauts use the bathroom?" Rosie said, laughing.

"Of course," Martin said. "I just preferred to use the scientific term."

"We try our best to keep a sense of humor," Rosie told Martin, "and to use plain language when we can. Yes, lots of science and technology went into figuring out how to let astronauts function in orbit in the easiest way possible. We use a flush system very similar to flush toilets here on Earth, and our bathroom space is private. But we have one advantage when we take sponge baths — we get to use a water gun!" Rosie explained how the gun can direct drops of water where they belong, rather than letting them pop aimlessly around the cabin.

Kacy was on cloud nine. She couldn't hear enough about how the mission worked, how the space shuttle lifted into orbit like a rocket, sailed around the Earth like a spaceship and floated back down to its Earth runway like a glider. Rosie brought a model of the ship with her, and showed the class how the two solid booster rockets helped propel the craft into space before they dropped back down to the ocean by parachute. She told them just how the giant external fuel tank helps fuel the orbiter's main engines and then separates from the shuttle and breaks up as it enters Earth's atmosphere. She explained that the orbiter housing the astronauts is pushed by its two systems engines right into low Earth orbit.

"All our experiments are performed in the orbiter," Rosie explained. "The back section becomes a giant space lab, ready for many types of experiments."

Kacy had a question. "How will you water my plant?"

"If we tried to water it the regular way, by pouring, there would be droplets floating all over," Rosie answered. "We'll have the water hosing hooked into the bottom of the plant so that pressurized water can spread upward into the dirt."

Kacy was listening so intently that she jumped when the bell rang. It *couldn't* be the end of the period — it seemed as though only five minutes had passed. She wanted to keep Rosie there forever, and she had lots more questions.

"Can you come back?" Sonya asked.

"Not in the near future," Rosie answered. "I have a few weeks here in Houston to get ready for our flight, and then I'll be assigned to the Kennedy Space Center in Florida to complete preparations for liftoff."

"Hurry, children, you'll be late for your next class," Mr. Wall said, ushering the front rows out.

"But we didn't get to clap, and we've clapped for lots worse speakers than this," Martin said. Kacy agreed.

"We certainly all thank Astronaut Ruiz for her wonderful visit," Mr. Wall said, "and let's clap as we go out the door."

Kacy thought this was so dumb. They should be doing something much better to show Rosie how much they liked her. At least she could clap the loudest, Kacy decided, so she threw her whole self into it.

In the middle of her clapping, Mr. Wall bent over and whispered into her ear, "You have a lot of responsibility for the school's name, Kacy. Perhaps you can keep control of yourself and not display some of the foolish behavior we've seen from you in the past. Ms. Harris doesn't know you as well as I do." Kacy felt her heart drop into her stomach, the way it always did when she received these little reminders from Mr. Wall. Reminders that she had blown things in the past and would probably do so in the future. She took a big breath, kept quiet, and decided not to let Mr. Wall ruin her day.

Ms. Harris led Rosie out of the class and into her office, and Kacy followed.

"Don't you have a class, Kacy?" Ms. Harris asked.

"Please, Ms. Harris, I have to talk to Rosie. She didn't even get to explain how my project will work."

"Don't worry, Kacy," Rosie said. She turned to Ms. Harris and said, "You know, Ms. Harris, it would be easier for me if I could speak to Kacy now about the arrangements, and perhaps you could stay, too, to help us work it out."

"You're right," Ms. Harris said. "All right, Kacy, you're in luck. Because you have such an important friend who's giving us her time, I'll let you be late for your next class."

30

Ms. Harris cleared room at her desk and the three of them sat around it. Ms. Harris took notes and suggested that Kacy do the same. Kacy was so glad she had worn her new vest — even more now that she was meeting with Rosie alone, or almost alone.

"Kacy, I think you might want to visit our facility once a week until I leave for Florida in about six weeks. I can arrange for our van to meet you at a NASA parking lot that's also used as a bus stop. There's a bus from Hobby airport here in Houston to Clear Lake, where NASA's located. If you don't mind taking two buses to get to us, and if your family okays it, we will meet you in our van every week to drive you directly to our lab."

"You mean I can be at NASA in your lab? *Me*? By myself, I mean? I mean, by myself with you there, of course?" Kacy was having a hard time controlling her voice. This wasn't real.

"Yes, I can let you tend your plant and make some photographs of it as it waits with the other experiments in the lab. By having it there for several weeks, we can get some baseline readings on it. And you can see how our lab operates. How does that sound to you?"

Kacy could not believe it, but she was getting the hiccups. Whenever she was really excited — not just ordinarily excited, but *really* excited — this stupid thing happened to her. Ms. Harris gave her a glass of water from a pitcher she kept right on her desk. She said between gulps and hiccups, "It sounds too good to be true, Rosie. I think I must be dreaming."

Ms. Harris, as usual, was planning ahead. "Kacy, there's a metro bus to Hobby airport within walking distance of school. Are you prepared for a long ride each week? Clear Lake and NASA are twenty miles south of downtown."

"Of course I'm ready! Metro bus fare doesn't cost much, either, and I already have a lot saved in my coin bank."

"Great!" Rosie said. "We'll check with your family

and see if it's all right for you to get home at about six o'clock once a week. How about Wednesdays? It'll take about an hour to get here, from three to four o'clock, with all the bus changes. You can stay with us for an hour, from four to five, and travel home from five to six. Someone can meet you at the bus stop."

"I know it'll be all right with Mom," Kacy said. "She gets home just before six." Her hiccups were beginning to subside.

"We can talk about the kind of plant on our first visit," Rosie said. "I'll look for you next Wednesday if your mom agrees. Why don't we exchange messages through you, Ms. Harris? Would you mind?"

"Of course not," Ms. Harris said. "I'll be the coordinator. Will you include me in the history books when you two get written up?"

Kacy's jaw dropped. This *was* a dream — she was sure of it. She, or at least her *plant*, might really have a place in a book about this flight.

"As soon as Ms. Harris tells me this is a *go*," Rosie said, using NASA language already, Kacy noticed, "I'll have an identification badge made up for you. When you get to the main gate, the van driver will see that you have a picture taken for an ID you can use for the whole time."

"We'll want to keep Mr. Wall posted on everything," Ms. Harris said. "I'm sure he'll be very helpful."

Kacy wasn't so sure, but she was certainly willing to hope so. He seemed to be happy having Rosie as a visitor to class, so maybe this whole thing would turn out to be smooth sailing. She made a vow to herself not to bring any more magazines to class to read under her books. She was turning over a new leaf. And who knows? Maybe Mr. Wall would quit picking on her. Even as she crossed all her fingers, she felt a little shudder of doubt. He'd made it pretty clear that he thought she'd make a mess of things.

A hand popped in front of her face. Rosie was about

32

to leave, and was putting out a hand for her to shake, in that cheerful, matter-of-fact way she had.

"Kacy, I'm looking forward to working with you."

Wow. Kacy's doubts were all cast aside. This was going to be something else. Something else indeed. Tom always said when you're handed the ball, forget everything else and run with it. Kacy was going to run with it. She shook Rosie's hand, and in a voice she hoped was as clear and optimistic as Rosie's, she said, "This is the best thing that ever happened to me. This might even change my life."

Later she would look back on this moment and realize she had no idea how true that was.

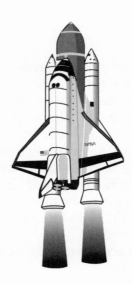

Chapter 6

A Badge
of Her Own

WEDNESDAY HAD FINALLY COME. Concentrating on schoolwork this week had been a real chore for Kacy, and she'd been waking in the middle of the night, wondering what she would find at Rosie's NASA laboratory. She had no trouble catching the bus to the airport after school, and the NASA van picked her up just where the bus had left her. In fact, the van was waiting for her.

"Hi!" the van driver greeted her. She was a woman who looked no older than Tom, though that couldn't be true. Kacy figured she was just a young-looking twenty-year-old. "You must be Kacy. I'm Tara." Tara wore a blue coverall with a NASA emblem on the pocket. She looked very official. "They tell me you'll be needing a badge for a few weeks."

"I'm really excited about it," Kacy told her, describing in detail everything that had happened to her during this incredible week. Then she stopped all of a sudden. "Tara, do you think I'm supposed to be talking about this? Maybe it's supposed to be a secret."

"I wouldn't worry about it if Dr. Ruiz hasn't said anything," Tara said. "I'm sure she'll fill you in on everything once we arrive."

"Dr. Ruiz? You mean she's a doctor? We just called her Astronaut Ruiz."

"Yes, she's a doctor. She has her Ph.D. degree — doctor of philosophy — in some scientific area, I think," Tara said. "With that degree, she can be called 'Doctor.'"

"Are you training to be an astronaut too?" Kacy asked.

"No, I'm just glad to have a good job," Tara said. "I have a little girl at home, and this job at NASA allows me to be a part of something exciting and earn a living too."

She must be older than she looked. Kacy wondered if she were a single parent like her own mom, but she decided not to ask. She looked out the window and realized they'd been on the Gulf Freeway for a long time, and to her surprise, the NASA 1 highway was in the distance.

Kacy had worn some good jeans, her cleanest gym shoes, and a checkered shirt. Ms. Harris had thought that was a good choice. She would be ready for work no matter what assignment she had. Maybe she'd even have some climbing around to do, but that was just a wild guess.

Kacy had forgotten that getting an ID badge meant having her picture taken. She had her red hair tied in a ponytail to keep it out of the way. She hoped she wouldn't look like a boy in the photo with her hair pulled away from her face. Tara thought she looked just fine.

As soon as the van dropped her off at the main gate, a man met her and took her into a small building close to the gate. When the photo session was done, Kacy found Tara waiting by the gate in the van.

"They didn't even ask me to say 'Cheese,'" Kacy said.

On the way to Rosie's building the van passed a big Saturn rocket, one of those left over when the last Apollo flights were canceled, before Kacy was born. Just seeing it there gave her a thrill. What was it about roaring up into space that was so exciting to her? Her van driver

Tara admitted that she, too, was hopelessly nuts over space travel.

Rosie was waiting outside the lab when the van pulled up. Kacy stepped out and shook her hand. Tara promised to pick Kacy up in one hour.

"Welcome to Lab 59," Rosie said. "We have a lot to do in an hour." She led Kacy into the three-story building that was much plainer than Kacy had imagined. Some neat pictures of previous space flights were on the hallway walls, though.

"This is a working lab building," Rosie said, as if she had sensed what Kacy was thinking. "There are no fancy offices for us here."

"It looks a little bit like pictures I've seen of military bases," Kacy said.

"Well, military personnel work here, too, and we have many military contracts to deal with," Rosie said.

Rosie motioned Kacy ahead of her into a big laboratory with long tables laid out in rows. Several women and men in lab coats looked up and smiled at Kacy.

"These are my friends and co-workers, Kacy." Rosie introduced her to Teddy, Marsha, Andy, and Joan. Joan had a ponytail, like Kacy's, and Marsha wore some very cool-looking glasses pushed on top of her hair for when she needed them. Teddy was always making jokes, Rosie said, and Andy was quiet, but the hardest worker. They looked as if they were in their twenties, a bit younger than Rosie. She had told Kacy she was thirty. A baldheaded custodian was cleaning up some spilled bottles in one corner of the lab, and he was introduced to her as Sam.

All Rosie's friends at the lab were working on experiments to be placed aboard the space shuttle *Discovery,* which was to go into orbit in a few months. They invited Kacy to sit down at a round table by a small refrigerator.

"Sodas all around," Rosie said. Kacy liked this way of working. "I thought you might tell us your ideas about the plant you want to put into orbit. What species did you have in mind?"

Kacy was feeling overwhelmed by the sight of NASA scientists sitting down and listening to *her*, but she wasn't about to let them know she was scared. Just the thought of Mr. Wall's doubts about her spurred her on to put her best face forward. She was going to do this, and do it right. Her mom and Tom thought she could do it, and so did Bethany and Sonya. That was four against one. Five if she counted Ms. Harris, six if she counted Rosie, and seven if she counted herself. She felt better, and brought out some notes she had copied into her smallest spiral notebook.

"I thought I'd like a flowering plant like a daisy. It's sturdy, but it may grow taller than you have room for. Or do you think I should pick something kind of squat shaped, like a cactus?"

"There are smaller species of daisy," Rosie said, "and they do grow rapidly. Let's bring a plant into the lab and see how it grows here."

"And if the first daisy doesn't work all that well, we'll have plenty of time to try another kind," Kacy said.

"Would you like to look around the lab and see what we're planning for this next flight?" Teddy asked. He led Kacy around to each of the tables, where projects were being prepared and coordinated. Kacy learned that many of the experiments would be delivered to the lab just before flight time. They had been developed and nurtured by companies all over the world in their own laboratories before being sent to Houston. One project that had already arrived was an experiment involving the growth of protein crystals, which could be used in making medicines. Teddy was taking care of this project, and Rosie was supervising it. The project was also important to the government, and part of it was still secret.

"I'll be going down to the Kennedy Space Center in Cape Canaveral, Florida, in a few weeks," Rosie said. "Eleven weeks before our flight, we train there and begin to learn the exact specifications of our trip into orbit. Until then, as a mission specialist, I train here in Houston and learn every detail of our mission. There will be

EVA on this flight, too, if you remember my talking about that in class — extravehicular activity. Astronauts will be suiting up to go outside the orbiter in order to repair a satellite.

"We put our experiments onto pallets," she continued. "They can slide right into place with all the projects in their own special sections of the orbiter. Some crew members will be carrying out other plans."

Kacy liked that idea. Even though her mom thought she was messy, simply because of what her room looked like at any given moment, she didn't see herself as disorganized at all. She could put her hands on anything in her room she wanted, if no one had tried to clean or straighten it. And she thought she had an orderly mind — at least when she concentrated. She liked the fact that scientists have a place for everything, and that they have things under control.

"Will my daisy be on a pallet?" Kacy wondered.

"Yes, I've assigned it a place near one of the crystal experiments," Rosie told her. "Your pallet now and in orbit will be Number B-52."

"Wow! That's easy enough to remember. I think I'm lucky to have that one."

"Not lucky," Teddy leaned over to explain. "Rosie gave you that number on purpose. She thought you'd like it."

"Thanks, Rosie," Kacy said. She was amazed that, as busy as Rosie was, she had still taken time to think of something Kacy would like. Kacy had already begun to think of Rosie as a big sister. She knew from her talk to the class that Rosie was the youngest child of five brothers and sisters. She was the only one of the lot who had gone into science. Rosie was from Santa Fe, New Mexico, and had grown up in the shadow of the beautiful Sangre de Cristo Mountains, last of the Rockies. Rosie had said she missed those mountains when she went to graduate school in Massachusetts. She enjoyed being close to the Atlantic Ocean and vacationing on the Cape Cod seashore, but she said the mountains were her home.

Rosie took a piece of yellow lined paper and used a red marker to write down directions to Kacy for buying the daisy.

"Buy two, Kacy. Make sure they're well fertilized and that the potting mixture is rich. Choose the healthiest looking daisy plants you can find. They don't have to be in bloom. In fact, it's better if they bloom later. We'll be happy with very small plants for now. One can be the plant you keep here for comparison, and the other will go on the flight."

"How long will you be in space?" Kacy asked.

"Our mission is for twelve days," Rosie said.

"Oh, boy, a lot can happen in twelve days." Kacy thought of her daisy in orbit of the Earth for all that time. Would it change? Would its growth be stunted, or would it surprise all of them and grow in space to a giant size?

Rosie assured her that although anything could happen, it was unlikely the plant would do something "out of a space movie." They all laughed.

"But you never know," Teddy said, and winked at her.

Rosie seemed a little distracted today. She looked worried.
Kacy could see it in her eyes.

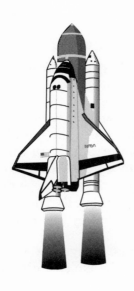

Chapter 7

The Crystal Project Jinxed?

SIX WEDNESDAYS HAD PASSED since Kacy's first visit to NASA. Today was Rosie's last Wednesday at the lab before being transferred to Cape Canaveral in Florida, for the remaining eleven weeks of her training before the launch. Kacy had brought a surprise. She had baked her special cookie-candy combination for the whole crew at the lab. The squares were in honor of Rosie's launch, and Kacy called them her "Space Yummies."

"These are delicious, Kacy," Andy said. "My two favorite treats — M&M's *and* cookies." As her new friends began to devour the whole pan full of goodies she had made for them, Kacy discovered she wasn't as hungry as she thought. She knew she would miss Rosie terribly.

Rosie had assured her she could still come to the lab each week and tend the duplicate daisy plant she was using to compare to the one which would fly in space. When the flight was over and Rosie returned to Houston, Kacy could come back to the lab for "wrap-up" sessions to find out how her plant had survived in orbit.

Rosie seemed a little distracted today. She looked worried. Kacy could see it in her eyes.

"What's the matter, Rosie?" she asked, as she finished up the Coke Rosie had jammed into her hand when she came into the lab later. The workers in the lab were Kacy's friends now, and she was comfortable with them. She had even stopped breaking into a sweat each time she entered that amazing room full of science experiments destined for space. Rosie was usually the most cheerful of the lot, and always seemed happy to see Kacy, but today she was unusually quiet.

"I'm not sure what the matter is, Kacy. One of the crystal experiments I'm responsible for isn't coming together. Just like in school, you know, some projects go well and others don't."

"Oh yeah, tell me about it," Kacy groaned. She knew all too well about school assignments that turned sour. "That's the story of my life. What's the experiment about?"

"It's a joint governmental-commercial project for growing protein crystals. We think they can be grown in a purer form in the weightless atmosphere of space. The better the structure of the crystal, the better the medicine or other product that can be made from it."

"What's the matter with it?" Kacy knew she asked a lot of questions, but so far the NASA crew had answered all of them without rolling their eyes to the ceiling like Mr. Wall did. And yes, she might as well admit it — her own mom did the same thing sometimes when she was busy.

"There are unexplained growth problems that shouldn't be happening this late in the project. According to the specifications we received from the people in Belgium who prepared this pallet, these crystals have been tested and retested. But the crystals are developing unevenly, and each time I think I have the problem fixed, it turns up again."

"Maybe someone's sneaking into the lab and changing things," Kacy volunteered.

"Kacy!" Marsha had been listening. "What an imagination!" She and Andy came over to her corner of the room and pretended to be shocked. Even Teddy threw her a strange look.

"No, I don't think so, kid," he said. "But I give you credit for a good try. Maybe we have space gremlins appearing after dark."

Rosie managed a little smile, but Kacy could tell she wasn't cheered by any of this. In fact, she gave Kacy a long look and shook her head. "I'm the mission specialist, and the work is under my control," she said. "I have wonderful help, but none of us has been able to prevent these random happenings. There are times when I almost believe the protein crystal project is jinxed."

Kacy kept quiet and tended her daisy. Her brother had warned her that her big mouth would get her into trouble someday, and she didn't want this to be the day. Her new friends in the lab probably already thought she was weird. But she made a promise to herself to be on the lookout for anything in the lab that didn't seem quite right. Someone had to pay attention, and the others were always so busy. Her hour a week was short, but she could still keep her eyes open. Who knew what might turn up?

Tara picked her up at the regular time, and dropped her off at the bus stop by the big parking lot outside the NASA gates. It was hot waiting in the sun, and Kacy had learned that the bus to Hobby airport was sometimes late. Wednesdays involved two bus trips each way, but her hour with Rosie was definitely worth it. Luckily, there were several buses leaving at different times from the airport to Kacy's house, so she never had to worry about missing one if her other bus was late. Mom had told Kacy when the project started that she expected her to report in often and keep up with her schoolwork. So far, so good. The new leaf she had turned over was working, and she hadn't been grounded or sent to Ms. Harris' office since the last incident with Mr. Wall.

Kacy sucked on a plastic water container her friends

in the lab had given her for these hot afternoon waits. It was blue with a permanent straw attached, and had "NASA" printed on one side. She wore a white baseball cap, also from the lab, because Rosie had said it wasn't healthy to stand in the Houston sun for too long a time. Sweat dripped from behind her ponytail down her back.

As she was standing there, making x's with her toe as part of a tic-tac-toe game in the dirt, Kacy noticed a dirty green car headed through the far section of the parking lot — the part reserved for cars, not buses.

She'd noticed the car there before but hadn't paid much attention. This time, it stopped to pick up a passenger, and although she couldn't see well that far away, she recognized the person who was being picked up. It was Sam, the lab custodian. Kacy was sure because of his bald head shining in the sun and his stooped shoulders. She couldn't see who was driving.

The car roared out of the opposite end of the lot, making lots of old-car engine noise. Tom would have said the motor hadn't been tuned in a long, long time. Kacy waved, but it was probably too late for Sam to have seen her. Besides, he was going the other way.

She wondered if he would have waved back if he'd seen her. Sam did his cleaning with his head down most of the time, and she'd never noticed him talking with the workers, either. He was only in the lab for the first part of her hour, and then he always left. She supposed he was off duty at that time, though she had never had any reason to ask. Or care, for that matter. She reminded herself to tell him next Wednesday that she'd seen him. It would give her something to talk to him about, since she hadn't gotten to know him very well.

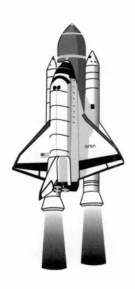

Chapter 8

That Mysterious Dirty Green Car

KACY TOLD SONYA and Bethany what Rosie had said about the crystal project being jinxed — or just *maybe* being jinxed. Mom said she was always jumping to conclusions, so Kacy tried not to exaggerate too much. It was part of the new leaf stuff, and she really was trying to be better. When Bethany came to the house to spend the night, she brought a tape recorder with her.

"You can plant it somewhere," she said.

"Sure, Bethany."

"No, I mean it. Why not try it?"

"Because it's stupid. The tape would run out, and someone would find it, anyway. The lab's not like your room, Bethany. They know where everything is there."

She did promise Bethany she'd let her know if anything suspicious turned up, and sure enough, it did. On her very next visit to NASA.

As soon as she entered Lab 59 and had her Coke, Kacy went over to talk to Sam.

"Hi, Sam." She thought she'd start slow because he'd

never paid attention to her, and she thought she might have to introduce herself all over again.

Sam looked up from his broom and dustpan. Kacy thought he made a faint grunt, but she wasn't sure. She guessed his looking up was as much attention as she was going to get. But, being herself, she wasn't ready to give up yet.

"Remember me? I'm Kacy."

She thought he said, "How ya doin'," but it was pretty muffled and she wasn't sure. It might have been "Whaddaya doin'." She went ahead on the theory he said "Whaddaya doin'," because that required an answer, and she wanted to talk.

She'd never been particularly shy, but this was hard. Should she say, "I saw you being picked up last week?" No, that sounded dumb. She had to think of something else.

"Hey, I saw you in a green car. Is that a friend of yours?"

Sam dropped his dustpan.

Sometimes when she was trying to be the most careful, she made the biggest fool of herself. Her brother had warned her about that. She remembered something else Tom had told her — if you mess up, take a breath and start over. She started over.

"Uh, I didn't mean was the car a friend of yours, even if that's what it sounded like. See, last Wednesday, I saw you being picked up after work in the parking lot, and I tried to wave to you but you didn't see me. I was just making conversation about whether that was a friend who picked you up."

Sam glanced back at her from his stooped position on the floor, where the dustpan had fallen. He looked at her as if she'd been speaking a foreign language.

Kacy noticed that the end of her red ponytail was automatically being twisted in her hand — her old nervous habit. She was really blowing this. She wondered if, by grown-up rules, she could be allowed to start over one more time. Probably not. She decided to forge ahead from where she left off.

"Maybe I'll see you again today," she said. Sam stood up. His shoulders didn't seem so stooped as he rose to full position. He was taller than Kacy thought, and then she remembered that whenever she had seen him before, he was bent over a broom or crouched on the floor. Yep, he was tall. And he didn't look very friendly, either.

"No, you must have been mistaken. No green car picked me up." He looked down and directly at her as he said it, and he didn't mumble.

"A dirty green one? Maybe it was like an olive color with the dirt. I don't always get my colors right. Yellow-ish green."

"No car picked me up." He picked up his broom and dustpan and left the room. Just like that. The others were busy working, and Kacy was glad. The whole thing had been embarrassing.

Kacy reported the entire conversation to Bethany and Sonya when she got home. She just wasn't ready to be hassled by Tom about it. He was great on the big things, but he drove her crazy teasing her about the little things.

"Suspicious. Definitely suspicious behavior," Sonya said.

"But there's nothing I can do, is there? Sam seems to be part of the group. I just have to keep watching."

"You never were very patient," Sonya said, "but in this case, I don't know what else you can do. Just hang in there."

Sonya was right, and Kacy decided to just hang loose during her trips to the lab. It wasn't half as much fun now that Rosie was gone, and there wasn't really that much to do. Both daisy plants were growing nicely, and Kacy spent a lot of time deciding which one would be the lucky one to make the trip in the space shuttle. The pallets of scientific experiments would be collected a few days before the liftoff date and flown down to the Kennedy Space Center in Florida.

47

Teddy and the others thought of things Kacy could do to keep occupied — probably so she would stay out of their hair, Kacy imagined. They were all very busy during these last weeks, and she tried hard not to disturb them. She rearranged some equipment in the lab, and was allowed to watch while Andy and Marsha recorded updates on the crystal protein experiments. Once, while Kacy was at the lab, Rosie actually spoke to her by phone on one of her project update calls. Rosie spoke to the others several times a week and they were used to it, but Kacy was thrilled to hear Rosie's voice all the way from Florida.

"Rosie, I'm going to watch your liftoff and record the whole thing on our VCR at home," Kacy told her.

"Great, Kacy. And you can think of your daisy coming along with me."

"Are you scared?" Kacy knew this sounded foolish, but she just had to ask it.

"A little. Sitting on the nose of a rocket can be a bit nerve-wracking if you stop to think about it too much, and yet, that's exactly how our space shuttle is positioned, Kacy."

"I don't know if I'd have the nerve, Rosie."

"Don't forget, Kacy, we've been training for this for years. I wouldn't miss this chance for anything. You shouldn't worry about me. Just send me good vibes."

"I'll keep wishing you good luck," Kacy assured her. She privately told herself she'd try not to be nervous.

Kacy wished Sam would show the same good feelings as the rest of them. She knew he just considered his job a cleanup job, and didn't spend time getting involved with the scientists, but she pictured herself in the same job, and knew she'd be excited even to work there as a custodian. She realized she hadn't seen Sam lately, and wondered if he had been avoiding her since their conversation. Something about him — well, *everything* about him — just didn't sit well with her.

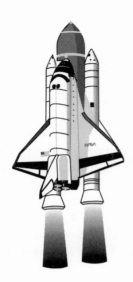

Chapter 9

Kidnapped!

KACY SAT NEXT TO the bus window and pressed her nose to the glass, trying to see how close she was to NASA and the lab. The bus was zipping along at a remarkable speed, considering the fact that it was tunneling through one of the heaviest downpours ever to hit Houston. The city, in swampland territory and so close to the Gulf, was used to torrential rains that swept through and took over. The bayous often overflowed, but these sideways pellets of water were fierce even for Houston. The rain had been thick and steady since last night, and Mom, worried that the streets would be flooded, almost hadn't let her go today. Kacy had to be her most persuasive to be allowed to make the trip at all.

Today, of all days, was not one Kacy wanted to miss. This was her last Wednesday in the lab before liftoff, and her last chance to check on her daisy. Tonight the pallets would be packed, sealed, and shipped to Florida. Thursday they would be loaded into the shuttle. Friday was liftoff.

"Mom," Kacy had wailed that morning at breakfast, "you just *have* to let me go. The future of the whole daisy mission depends on me. What if I have to report something wrong with my plant?"

Tom sniffed, turning his back to her as he read the sports page of the newspaper and ate a bagel. "Don't you think this kid is getting just a tad carried away with herself?" he said. "You'd think we were living with our very own mission specialist. Does this astronaut Rosie know her job is in danger of being taken over by Kacy the Space Cadet?"

Kacy kicked him hard under the table. "Not now, you toad," she whispered. "I need you to get her to let me go."

Tom did point out to Mom that if the streets were flooded, the bus company would know about it and cancel the schedule.

"OK, honey," Mom finally said. "I know you want to be there on the day before your experiment is flown down to Florida. Just be careful. And check with the bus driver to make sure they think the roads are safe. If the driver shows the slightest hesitancy, I want you to catch the other bus home and stay off the highway. Oh — and take your folding umbrella in your backpack."

"I promise, Mom."

Kacy hugged her mom and, on an impulse, hugged Tom too. She would think about that many hours later.

For now, as she sat on the bus and opened a granola bar Mom had given her, she thought the driver was doing just fine handling the slick highways. He had told her the bus was equipped with special tires that gripped the road in wet weather, and Kacy knew Mom would like hearing that.

The bus arrived at the NASA lot in no time. She opened her red folding umbrella and stepped off the bus into the rain, which had died down a little. She quickly headed for the covered bus stop to wait. Tara's van wasn't scheduled to arrive for twenty minutes. The rain made everything dark and kind of depressing, and Kacy was in a hurry to get into the bright, dry corridors of the lab building.

After the bus had pulled away, Kacy noticed a familiar car pull into the parking lot. It was the dirty green car. The first thing she thought was, "So it *wasn't* my imagination." She hadn't seen the car for weeks, and Kacy had almost begun to doubt she had ever seen Sam being picked up. Maybe it was someone just like him. After all, the car had been all the way across the lot each time she had noticed it. The green car had always made its appearance *after* her hour at the lab, not before. Yet here it was, before her hour at the lab — at the wrong time and in the wrong place.

This time, instead of parking on the other side of the lot, the woman driver was headed right toward the covered bus stop where Kacy stood holding her closed umbrella. Kacy could make out a passenger in the front seat and one in the back. As the car came closer, she recognized Sam sitting in the front seat. A woman with a scarf covering her head and tied under her chin sat in the back seat. To Kacy's surprise, the car pulled up right in front of her, and Sam rolled down his window.

"Would you like a ride?" he said.

Sam actually smiled at her. This had never happened before. He almost looked pleasant. Kacy gave a little smile back, happy that Sam was at least decent to someone standing in the rain. It was a kind offer, even if he did look as creepy as ever. When he smiled he showed brown teeth, probably from the cigar he was smoking.

Since she knew Sam was going to the lab, a very small part of Kacy was tempted to take up his offer. After all, it wasn't as if he were a stranger. The lab *was* close by, and she *was* getting soggy from the rain coming in sideways.

She stood there for a moment, fidgeting with her umbrella. All of a sudden, the thought hit her that this made no sense — no sense at all. When she had asked that day, Sam had told her he had never been picked up in a green car. Now, here he was, sitting in the same passenger seat where she had seen him each of those times after work.

Think, she told herself. She saw Tom's face before her saying, *Use your noodle, Kace.*

And why was he being so nice to her? None of this

The woman, her scarf covering her head,
jumped out of the car before Kacy ever saw she was coming.

added up. What had Sonya said? *Definitely suspicious behavior.*

Kacy came up with an answer fast. "Thanks, anyway," she said, "but Tara's van will be here to get me any minute. She'd be worried about me if I didn't show up."

In case they *were* up to no good, maybe the idea of the van coming would scare them off. Besides, Tara *would* be worried.

"We'll tell the people at the lab," Sam said. "It's no problem." He was being very nice, but Kacy's spine was tingling. She stood her ground very politely while he tried to persuade her, but she had already decided she would definitely wait for Tara's van.

Kacy was concentrating on Sam with all her might. What she couldn't notice, though, was that at the same time Sam was talking to her, the woman in the back seat was quietly and quickly opening the back door of the car. The woman, her scarf covering her head, jumped out of the car before Kacy ever saw she was coming. She grabbed Kacy from the back and, with the strongest arms Kacy had ever felt, lifted her off the ground and into the back seat. Kacy struggled and jabbed at her with the umbrella, but the woman managed to close the door anyway. With the last bit of strength Kacy had, she threw her umbrella out the open window, pushing on the latch so that it fell out, opened, onto the parking lot.

The thought flashed through Kacy's mind that maybe Tara would see the umbrella and know something awful had happened to her. The woman, much heavier and stronger than Kacy, tied Kacy's arms in front of her and took off her own scarf to use as a blindfold for Kacy.

"Good! Let's get out of here," Kacy heard Sam say as they sped away.

The storm came up in force again. Kacy could not know that her red umbrella, caught in a sudden gust of wind and rain, had flipped inside out and was blown far away from the parking lot, like a forlorn kite lost in a gale.

Tara would never see it.

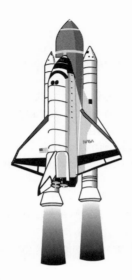

Chapter 10

The Suspicious Hamburger

KACY TRIED TO SCREAM, but Sam and the two women all yelled at once, "Shut up!" It sounded so scary, she shut up. Besides, she realized the car was speeding so fast no one would hear her. Her heart was pounding, and her blindfold was getting wet. Apparently, you could cry tears even with your eyes shut tight by a scarf. She felt sick to her stomach too.

"Listen, girl," Sam said in what Kacy thought was a very mean voice, "listen up good. We're taking you somewhere to spend the night. If you do everything we say and keep quiet, we'll keep you safe and sound. You got that?"

"But I want to call my mom *now*."

"Did you hear the 'keep quiet' part? You can't call your mother. If you want us to call and tell her you're OK, you have to shut up and follow orders. Then we'll see."

"But I'm *not* OK!"

"OK, then we won't have to call her, will we?" Kacy could hear that Sam was as cranky as ever. She tried to talk to the woman beside her, who was sitting in the middle of the back seat and had her wedged into a corner by the door.

"Why am I here?" Kacy turned her head toward the woman.

"Shut up."

"Let her talk, Donna," came a voice from the front seat. It was the woman who hadn't spoken yet. "I'm the one who's going to be watching her and I don't want a hysterical child on my hands. We can keep her from being so scared."

"Then you answer, Miss Child Expert."

"I'm Cheryl. I hear your name's Kacy."

The voice from the front seat sounded a lot better than the other two. Kacy decided to stick with her.

"I want my mom! I feel like I need to throw up the granola bar I ate on the bus." Kacy felt Donna move away from her fast. She hadn't planned it this way, but now she realized she had more room to breathe.

"Just settle down," Cheryl told her. "Take some breaths. You'll feel better."

It didn't look as though they would stop the car for her to throw up, or even care, so Kacy tried to hold it in. She wondered what to do next. Once, a long time ago, she, Sonya and Bethany worked out a plan to send ESP messages to each other by mind control if any one of them were in danger. She tried it, but knew in her heart she'd better not count on one of them receiving it.

On TV mysteries a kidnapped person could always tell where the car was headed by listening, but all Kacy could hear was rain on the windows. They seemed to drive for ages, but then again, it might not have been very long. She couldn't really tell. Her stomach felt better when she was quiet, so she just sat there and tried to think. She was also a little worried that they'd gag her mouth if she talked any more. She did notice they didn't stop for stoplights, so maybe they were on the freeway.

She hadn't felt them slowing down for any exits, but

all of a sudden, they slammed on the brakes and stopped. Now she was really scared. What if they were stopping to bump her off? She and Bethany had just been discussing a movie where — no, she wasn't going to do this. Cheryl didn't sound as if that was going to happen. She had talked about taking care of a hysterical child, so she must be planning to take care of her, at least for now. It wouldn't do any good to believe the worst. Tom's face flashed in front of her. *Hang in, Squirt.*

Donna got out of the car and pulled Kacy out with her. Kacy stumbled and almost fell.

"Pick her up, Donna," Cheryl said. "It'll be easier and faster."

Donna was strong — Kacy could tell that from before when she had grabbed her from the parking lot. Donna was rough, but Kacy was glad Sam hadn't decided to pick her up. She was even more afraid of him.

She felt herself being carried just a few steps to what must have been a door. Someone pulled it open and it creaked. It sounded heavy, and not like the front door to a house. The footsteps of her three thugs, as she called them (courtesy of Tom, who watched James Cagney movies a lot on cable), echoed off the floor. Their voices sounded hollow, too, so this must be a very big room or large space of some sort.

They walked for a long time until finally Donna put Kacy down. She couldn't stand up — her knees just wouldn't do it — so she slipped down to a cold floor and started crying again.

"Take her blindfold off," Cheryl said.

Kacy blinked and wiped at her eyes with her fingers. She looked up at the three of them, standing in a circle around her. Sam looked the way he always did — mean and dorky. Donna was older than Mom, maybe forty, and her brown hair was pulled back in a knot. She had a very stocky body — it looked just the way it had felt. Cheryl was younger than Mom, but much older than Tom, so she must have been twenty-something. She was kind of

56

medium tall, and thinnish. She had blond hair that looked as if it were streaked with two light colors. Of the three, she definitely had the nicest look on her face. Kacy didn't want to look at the other two. They scared her. She decided to do all her talking with Cheryl, which seemed to be fine with the other two, anyway.

"What are you going to do with me? Why do you have me?"

"You don't need to know why we have you, and we aren't going to hurt you. We have your phone number and we'll call your family," Cheryl told her.

"How can I know you'll do it?"

"Well, Missy, I guess you can't," Sam said. "But we said we'd do it and we will, especially if you'll behave and not give us trouble."

Cheryl lifted Kacy up and Sam led them into a small room, divided into two parts by a steel gate. The gate reminded Kacy of the metal accordion grating used to lock glass storefront show windows, in neighborhoods where store owners were afraid of thieves breaking in after business hours. The gate opened and closed by sliding back and forth, like the old-timey elevator doors in movies Kacy had seen on TV. The openings in the grating were big enough to stick your arm through, she noticed. Kacy wondered if they had fixed up this divided room just to hold her prisoner. And why in the world would they want her as a prisoner?

Sam told Cheryl to put Kacy on the far side of the gate, and then he slid it closed and locked it. Kacy figured they must be in some kind of warehouse. The place was like a big, cold cavern, with cement floors and high ceilings. At least the little room was warmer. It had one window, and Kacy thought maybe she could climb out of it, though it was high up and she had no idea how she would do it. There were no chairs in her part of the room, and Cheryl told her to sit on the floor.

"OK, Sam, why don't you go call her mom and leave her to me for a while?" Cheryl suggested.

"What will Sam tell my mom?" Kacy asked when he had left. "I wish you were calling her."

"We thought Sam should call her because he's connected with the lab. He'll tell her it has something to do with the launch this week, and that you'll be staying at the lab with all the workers while they prepare for the flight. She won't worry."

"Yes, she will." That story made no sense, anyway. Kacy knew the lab would be calling her mom when she didn't show up. "How long are you going to keep me here?" she asked.

"Not more than two days, Kacy. I've brought you two things to keep you more comfortable." Cheryl stayed on the outside of the gate and handed through a small blanket from a large paper bag. She pushed the blanket through the diamond-shaped openings in the grating until it fell into Kacy's side of the room. From the bottom of the bag, she pulled out, of all things, a Big Mac.

"We brought some food along with us. Hope you like hamburgers."

Kacy didn't answer. She was in no mood to eat anything now.

"If you're not hungry now, keep it for later, but don't wait too long because it will spoil and you're going to be hungry sooner or later. We're not planning to bring in more food before tomorrow. I suggest you eat it now. I'll bring you a cup of water soon and check back to see how you're doing."

"Can I have something to read?"

"Maybe — if you eat your hamburger."

Why does she care whether or not I eat it? Kacy wondered to herself when Cheryl had gone. Still, it might be worth forcing it down to get something to read. Maybe whatever they brought her to read would give her some clue as to who they were or where she was.

She decided to eat the Big Mac. It smelled all right, and the bun was still soft — a good sign. Of course, as usual, she had to open it and take it apart. She remembered Tom and Mom hassling her about picking through her beans and rice. If she could just see them, she'd never mind their badgering her ever again. She might even decide to stop picking at her food before eating it. But that was later, and this was now, and she wasn't about to change her habits in this place.

She opened the wrapper and laid aside the top bun half. Then she looked at the cheese, lettuce, pickle, sauce, and meat. She didn't want any lettuce today. She didn't exactly hate it, but she liked Mom's better than this wet lettuce. She picked every single piece of lettuce off the hamburger meat. Then she saw it. In between the cheese and the lettuce — not much bigger than a piece of relish, and the same color as the white pieces of lettuce, was a tiny, round, seed-sized thing that didn't look like anything else. She carefully picked it up and, with her good jet pilot eyesight, she saw writing on the tiny front of it. *A pill!*

Kacy thought fast. This must be a knockout pill. She remembered a rerun of *Murder She Wrote* where Jessica goes to a party and discovers a pill in some shrimp dip — right on top of the potato chip she was getting ready to put into her mouth. Jessica worked it around into her cheek and then spat it out later. Bethany had been watching the show with her, and they had talked about what a cool maneuver it was.

She didn't need to keep it in her cheek, though, because no one was watching. Kacy put the tiny pill in her shirt pocket and buttoned the pocket. She was glad she'd worn the blue oxford one with the button-down stuff. Despite the fact that she was pretty damp from the rainstorm, the pocket seemed dry enough. Then she took a deep breath, and slowly began to eat the hamburger. Slowly, just in case her stomach felt weird again. Before she took each bite, she looked for more pills, but she found no more.

Eating was probably a good idea, since she would need all her strength for whatever was to come. Besides, the next meal might be something she hated, and at least this was something she could stand.

Kacy felt a bit better now. Finding the pill gave her hope that she could protect herself. What would her family say *now* about her picky food habits?

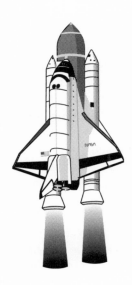

Chapter 11

Mission in Danger

KACY PLANNED TO pretend she was sleeping if Cheryl came in to check on her. Since she had supposedly been given a knockout pill, the kidnappers would certainly expect her to be knocked out by this time. And she knew she had to fake it until she could find out what was going on.

She stretched out on the worn blanket, trying not to notice its musky odor, like the smell of old sneakers. Still, it was better than lying on the cold cement floor, and she was grateful for it. She thought about her warm comforter at home, with the little scotty dog patches on it and the fresh smell from the dryer. She especially wished she had her favorite animal — the furry stuffed cocker spaniel her dad had given her when she was a baby. It looked just like a real light golden blond spaniel, and was still her favorite after all these years. She always hugged it in bed at night, and played with it only when her hands were clean— something that would have surprised Mom and Tom, since she usually had to be reminded about washing up.

Thinking about home and bedtime almost put her to sleep, but fortunately, one part of her stayed alert. She quickly shut her eyes after glimpsing Cheryl's blond hair when the door opened into her tiny room. She heard or felt or somehow sensed Cheryl walking around the front of the gate, and she kept her eyes closed in case Cheryl was bending over to see her. The next thing she heard was the door close as Cheryl left the room. Kacy carefully opened her eyes, then wiggled around in the dark since Cheryl had turned the light off, and finally rolled over close to the gate to see if she could hear anything.

She was in luck. The whole group seemed to be gathered in the other room, and she heard the rustle of paper bags. Food was being passed around, probably hamburgers too — but without pills inside, of course.

"She's out cold," Kacy heard Cheryl tell the others. "I'm worried about that sleeping pill, though. It's not child-sized, and who knows how deeply it will put her out? I'm afraid it could make her really sick."

"Quit worrying so much, will you?" Sam could always be counted on to be the meanest. Kacy thought he could be the most dangerous, and knew she had to watch out for him. "I'm more worried that she's seen our faces."

"But we talked about that," Cheryl said. "You said she would take the ride you offered her because she knew you, so you had to show her your face, right? And besides, if we're skipping the country, what difference does it make? Our boss wants us to report directly to him in Rome. We'll be on a plane before she ever wakes up from the sleeping pill we give her on Friday. It won't matter, then, what she says, and besides, she knows nothing of our plans."

Donna's voice piped up next. "I've gotta hand it to you, Cheryl. Your idea of the hamburger really worked — I'd never have thought of the Big Mac."

"All kids love fast food. It was no big deal," Cheryl said. Listening to her, Kacy had the feeling that Cheryl didn't really like Donna and Sam so much. She wondered what that would mean.

"I think we've taken too many chances already," Cheryl said. "We can't take her back now, but I'm sorry we did it in the first place."

"You know why it had to be done," Sam said. "Today is Wednesday. There was no way I could let her come to the lab today. I had to have her out of the way so the plan could go forward. Tonight they'll be packing up the whole pallet, and all the experiments will be flown to Florida tomorrow. Friday is the day of the launch. Kacy has to be kept quiet until the space shuttle is in orbit and the crystal experiment is spoiled. Of course, no one will know how it failed. They will think it simply didn't work."

Kacy almost cried out when she heard Sam say the crystal experiment would be spoiled. How? Why? And why wouldn't they want her to go to the lab today? She felt clammy and cold pressed up next to the door, but she knew she had to listen carefully. It was a lucky thing she had a good memory. She'd need to concentrate and remember everything that was said. She had trouble remembering boring stuff in class, but she never forgot anything that she absolutely *had* to remember.

Sam was still doing most of the talking. He must be the boss, or at least the boss of these two.

"I had to put the sealed packet into Kacy's plant early this morning, before the others arrived. There was too much chance of discovery later. I didn't want to be caught with it on me, either, so it had to be done this morning. By tonight, the pallets will be packed and sealed for tomorrow's flight to the launching site."

"But couldn't you have diverted Kacy?" Cheryl asked.

"Divert Kacy? *Ha!* You obviously don't know Kacy. She digs around in that plant the whole time she's there — pressing it and fooling with it and even talking to it."

And why shouldn't I talk to it? Kacy thought. She almost felt like bursting through the door to defend herself. Everyone knows the best gardeners talk to plants, and the good vibes help them to grow. Their neighbor

Jack talked to his squash plants and had the best crop ever. But what did digging around in her plant have to do with the mess she was in now?

She soon found out, when Sam explained the plan to Donna, who knew about the scheme but not the details. Sam told Donna that he had tried other methods of destroying the crystal experiment, but that those had proved to be too dangerous, because Rosie had begun to notice when things went wrong. Sam was afraid of being found out too soon, so he decided to make sure the experiment was wrecked after it was already in orbit.

"The sealed packet contains a poisonous chemical formula which will cause the protein crystals in the mission's main experiment to wither and die," Sam told her. "The packet is programmed to begin leaking on Saturday, a day after the shuttle reaches orbit of the Earth. I have planted the poison deep into the dirt of Kacy's plant, which is packed in the same pallet as the chief crystal experiment."

Kacy felt dizzy when she heard Sam's words. *Poison?* Rosie would be tending those experiments. She could breathe in the poison, or touch it when she examined Kacy's plant. There was no telling what could happen. Rosie's life could be in danger. Kacy was so upset over the news that she had no time to remember that she, too, was in grave danger.

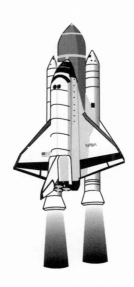

Chapter 12

Keep Your Eye
on the Ball

KACY TOSSED AND TURNED all night. She was afraid to be too active for fear Cheryl would open the door suddenly and discover she was awake. She definitely didn't want to be given another sleeping pill. The dopes, as she had begun calling them to keep up her spirits, had brought a TV set into the building to pass the time, she supposed, and it was loud enough to keep her from sleeping. But, in a weird way, the sound of it was comforting. It made her feel that somewhere out there, the world was going on with its business.

The next day, Thursday, was no better than the night before. Her thoughts were on the pallet being flown down to Florida. She felt like a caged animal imprisoned in the small locked room, and all the while she wanted to *do* something to stop the disaster. She was given very little food — just some cold cereal and powdered milk, which she hated. Though she picked and picked, she could find no pills hidden in the cereal.

She had the whole day to think, since the reading material they brought her consisted of one section from a year-old Sunday paper. The temptation was to feel scared and sorry for herself, but Kacy realized she must aim her ideas in a different direction. *Keep your eye on the ball*, Tom always said. The ball told her time was growing short. It sounded as though they were keeping her locked up at least until Friday's launch. If she could only warn Rosie somehow. Her gut told her that tomorrow, Friday, was her only chance. Chance for what? She wasn't sure. Kacy knew she didn't trust everything Sam was telling the others. Maybe instead of getting on the plane for Rome and then arranging for Kacy to be let loose, Sam was really planning to do away with her first and then leave the country.

As Thursday wore on, the beginning of a plan had begun to hatch in her mind. When Cheryl came in at suppertime and handed her a hamburger bag, Kacy realized she'd better take advantage of some conversation now, since as soon as she ate she was expected to fall asleep for the night. No doubt there was another pill in the hamburger.

"Cheryl, will all of you be here tomorrow too?"

"I'll be here, Kacy. Sam and Donna have some arrangements to make. But you won't be here alone."

"Did Sam call my mom?"

"Yes, I'm sure he did, just like he told you. Your mom won't worry — she knows the lab is very busy before the countdown for the shuttle flight."

Part of Kacy wanted to believe Sam had called Mom; the other part knew he hadn't. She decided to go with the first part, since the second would only hold her back for now. Last winter Kacy and her mom had found themselves driving on an icy road. Mom told her that if the car started sliding on the ice, the best thing to do was to turn the wheel in the direction of the skid — that to try and reverse the wheel to hold back the skid was the worst thing they could do. Believing Sam had called Mom was like that, Kacy thought. It might give her a push in the right direction when she needed it. She'd worry about what the truth was later.

"Since Sam won't be here tomorrow, could we watch the liftoff together? I've worked really hard all year to have my science experiment go up in space, and I promised Rosie I'd watch and wish her luck. It would mean a lot to me."

"Maybe it could be our secret," Cheryl said. "Sam said liftoff was at ten in the morning. I could bring the TV in here. He won't be back until after dark tomorrow."

Kacy thought the "after dark" part sounded creepy, but she couldn't spend much time thinking about it right now. She ought to show her appreciation. "Thanks so much, Cheryl. Really."

"I'd like to see the launch myself, and I might as well see it in here with you," Cheryl said.

"Can you bring burgers to have after the launch for an early lunch? It'll seem more like a celebration of the mission."

"OK, you've got a deal. Hamburgers are what you'll get."

"Will you have lunch with me?"

"Sure. In return, I want you to eat your supper now and get a good night's sleep before the shuttle takes off tomorrow. I'll be in the other room."

"Goodnight, Cheryl."

"Goodnight, Kacy."

Kacy gave a sigh of relief after Cheryl had gone. She took out the familiar Big Mac from the bag Cheryl had brought in. She was hungry since she hadn't eaten much cereal during the day, only the dry part.

Before she ate her hamburger, Kacy carefully inspected it. Sure enough, the pill was there, buried this time between the meat and the cheese, and nestled in the sauce. She dried it on the napkin and put it in her pocket with the pill from last night's supper. Then she took a contented bite of her burger, thinking all the while.

Yes, she felt better now. The first part of her plan was working.

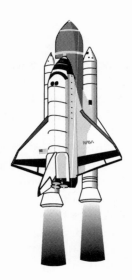

Chapter 13

Liftoff!

KACY SLEPT WELL FOR the first time since she had been kidnapped, and she awoke feeling more refreshed for the day to come, whatever that would bring. It was awful, though, not having even a sponge bath, and being hurried into a cramped bathroom by one of the dorks at odd times when she didn't even have to go. Usually Cheryl took her, carefully unlocking her gate and then locking it again when she had been brought back into the room.

Just as Cheryl had told her, Sam and Donna were gone when Kacy awoke this morning. Just before the liftoff was scheduled to begin, Cheryl came into her room and brought the small portable television set in with her. She set it up on her side of the accordion grating and raised the antenna as high as she could. Then she stepped back out into the other room and brought in another paper bag.

"The burgers you wanted," she said.

Kacy was on her best behavior. She didn't want Cheryl changing her mind. "I'm really glad we're watching together," she said. "Let's save our hamburgers for early lunch, OK?"

"Deal," Cheryl said. "I'm not exactly hungry in mid-morning."

The black-and-white set was hard to see, but Kacy wasn't complaining. She had expected to see the TV anchorperson first, but to her surprise, the network began with some footage taken only hours before, of the astronauts filing into the shuttle area to be suited up for the explosive bolt into space. There was Rosie! She had a big smile on her face, and she waved. Kacy told herself Rosie was waving to her. She was so excited, she actually forgot for a few moments that Rosie's mission was in danger. She remembered as soon as the cameras went live to the launchpad, but by then, she realized the countdown was the most important thing. Rosie needed to survive liftoff, first.

As exciting as it was, it was frightening, too, to think that her good friend was sitting on top of a gigantic firecracker ready to roar into space. The human beings atop that rocket were very, very small compared to the huge space shuttle. Its fuel tank was as big as half a football field, its booster engines set to fire into orbit.

Liftoff was about to begin. Kacy had a vision of her plant, placed neatly into the orbiter's mid-deck area, and ready to go into Earth orbit after all these weeks of waiting. She felt a sense of pride that she had, with Rosie's help, made this possible. For a few moments, she would not let herself think of the mess she was in. Surely, she could have a few moments to celebrate.

Four, three, two, one . . . Liftoff! The orbiter's main engines ignited first, then the solid rockets blazed upwards and the giant structure lifted off its launching pad. Two minutes after liftoff, the solid rockets fell by parachutes into the ocean to be picked up for later use. As the fuel in the external tank, the biggest part of the shuttle, was used up, it, too, would be discarded and break up over uninhabited ocean. Two other engines then would inject the orbiter into low Earth orbit. At that point, Kacy realized, Rosie and the crew would be launched and ready to live and work in space for ten days.

"Please," Kacy said to Cheryl, "let's watch until the broadcast ends, even though we can't see the shuttle anymore." Now that Rosie was safely launched, Kacy's mind raced back to her important plan. Her very life depended on it, and maybe Rosie's too.

"Ready for our early lunch or late breakfast?" Cheryl asked. "Can you calm down enough to eat without upsetting your stomach?"

"I'm calming down," Kacy assured her.

Cheryl picked up the bag and passed a burger to Kacy through one of the spaces in the metal gate. She took out the other one for herself.

"Could we have a drink of water to go with this?" Kacy asked, hoping desperately that Cheryl would say yes. This was the most vital part of the plan.

"Sure," Cheryl said. She put down the hamburger and went out of the room to get the cups of water.

Kacy reached through the diamond shaped openings in the steel accordion grating and grabbed Cheryl's hamburger. She quickly took the two knockout pills from her shirt pocket and stuffed them into the center of Cheryl's Big Mac, only unfolding the top part of the wrapping. She felt the pills squash into the lettuce and sauce. Perfect. She smoothed back the wrapping and put the hamburger back on Cheryl's side of the gate with time to spare.

In another moment, Cheryl came back with the water.

"Thanks," Kacy said. "You've really been nice, Cheryl."

"You've been pretty brave yourself."

"Are you hungry?" Kacy asked.

"Starved."

Between bites, Kacy kept up a steady stream of chatter, telling Cheryl all about the plant and her idea to write to Rosie. She wanted to give Cheryl plenty of time to eat and swallow. Soon, to her relief, Cheryl's burger was all gone. Kacy had been nibbling at the bun part. She didn't think there would be a pill in her hamburger, since the other pills were both given at nighttime, but there was no use taking chances. Kacy talked a lot instead of eating, and she hoped Cheryl would just think she was excited. Now for the next step.

"Cheryl, I'm feeling a little scared," Kacy said. "Could you sit close to me and talk to me? I know it's silly, but I'm nervous this morning. I'm afraid Sam will come back and get rid of me. If we could sit back to back and both lean against our sides of the gate, I wouldn't feel so alone."

"Sam's not going to hurt you, Kacy. And he'll be gone until tonight, unless he happens to come back early for some reason." Cheryl eased herself over on the floor near Kacy, and they sat back to back.

"Tell me about when you were a little girl," Kacy said. "Where did you live?"

"I lived in the mountains," Cheryl said. "My family had a farm near Gatlinburg, Tennessee, and my brothers and I grew up playing in the foothills of the Smoky Mountains. It was beautiful there."

Kacy kept the conversation quiet and story-like, and she hoped Cheryl was relaxing and that the pills were digesting in her stomach. She worried that they wouldn't work as fast since they'd been taken with food, but there was nothing she could do about that. Part of her wondered if Sam would be back before anything happened, but she pushed that out of her mind for now.

Soon Kacy noticed that Cheryl's voice became a bit slurred, and she began speaking more slowly. She leaned heavily against the grating that was against Kacy's back. All of a sudden, Cheryl's body slipped down sideways. She slumped. Kacy turned around and looked at her. Sure enough, her eyes were closed and her mouth was partially open. She was sound asleep.

Kacy reached both her hands through separate spaces in the grating and tried to turn Cheryl around so that her jacket pockets were within reach. Sleep seemed to have made her very heavy, and she was hard to turn. Kacy's hands were sweating, and her heart was thumping so hard she thought it might break. Maybe this was what having a heart attack was like. She told herself how strong she was — how many times she had swung from the live oak at the end of her street, and how much arm-wrestling practice she'd had with Tom, even though she'd never won. Her arms seemed to gather strength, and eventually she turned Cheryl over in the right direction. She fished through one pocket and then the other, and hoped Sam was staying away until dark, as he had said.

Finally, her fingers felt the key, in the very bottom of Cheryl's pocket. She brought her hands carefully back through the grate, with the key in one fist. She had it! Kacy unlocked the gate, slid it open, then pulled Cheryl's sleeping body over to Kacy's own side of the room. Now she needed to make sure the thugs would mistake Cheryl for herself. She turned Cheryl to face the wall and covered her completely with the old blanket, folding her legs and her arms until she looked as small as possible under the blanket. Then she went to the other side of the room and locked the grating behind her, keeping the key. When the others came back and looked into the room, they would think they were seeing her instead of Cheryl, and this would give her more getaway time.

Kacy left the divided room and crept into the bigger room, where all of them had talked the other night. Thank goodness it was daylight and she could see to search for the way out. She ran through the warehouse, or whatever the place was, and tried the back door. As she had hoped, it wasn't locked from the inside. As she slipped out the door and ran for the bushes to hide herself, she remembered that she hadn't looked for any money in Cheryl's pockets. No time to turn back for that now.

The humid Houston air felt wonderful to her. She knew she had only been held for two nights, but it seemed like an eternity. She ran down the block, from bush to bush, wondering how far away she'd have to get before she felt safe from Sam and Donna. She avoided the street. They might come along in their car and see her. She hoped she hadn't made a circle around the building, just dashing in and out of the bushes. It was high noon and hot, and so far, no one was around. This seemed to be a warehouse area, but everyone was inside. She was glad. Soon she would want to find people, but she hadn't run far enough to feel safe yet.

Kacy ran two more blocks and came to a busier intersection. She had no idea what part of town this was, or how far she was from Houston or NASA. She spied a phone booth and made a run for it. She had no money, but she remembered she could dial the operator without a coin. Just to be sure no one could see her, Kacy slipped down to sit at the bottom of the phone booth, and took the mouthpiece down with her. When she heard the operator's welcoming voice, she felt good for the first time in two days. She was free!

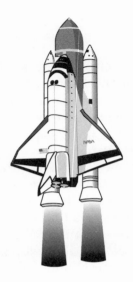

Chapter 14

A Close Call

KACY WANTED MOST of all to talk to her mom, but she decided she was still in danger and ought to call the police first.

"Speak up, please," the operator said. "I can't hear you."

"That's because I have to be quiet," Kacy said. "I'm in trouble and I need the police."

"I'll connect you right away."

The next words Kacy heard were, "Houston Police, Branch 37."

"I'm in trouble," Kacy repeated. "I've been kidnapped. I really want to speak to my mom but I figured I'd better — "

"Whoa, slow down," the voice said. "Your name, please."

Kacy gave her name and told where she lived. She was used to people telling her to slow down, and she realized she'd better be clear. Sam could drive by at any minute.

"You won't hang up on me, will you?" She was worried that she would have to start all over again, like the time she tried to call to get the cable fixed and had to repeat her story to four different people before someone would help her. This time, she might not have a second chance. It was hot in the bottom of the phone booth, she was tired and thirsty, and her feeling of freedom was slipping away fast.

"I guess you can hear from my voice that I'm a kid, but I'm not playing a joke or anything. I really am in trouble, mister, and this is pretty urgent." She wished she had said "sir" to a policeman instead of "mister," but it was too late to change that now.

"I'm here. I'm not going to hang up," the voice said. "Where are you calling from?"

"A phone booth, but I don't know where it is. I only know it's a few blocks from the place they took me to. I got away and . . ." Kacy stopped in midsentence, figuring she was going too fast again. She waited for the voice on the other end to catch up. She hadn't gotten any help yet, but so far, it was definitely better than the cable company.

"Hold on. I won't hang up. I'm getting my sergeant on the line."

Uh-oh, she spoke too soon. Now she'd probably have to start all over again.

It took forever to wait for the sergeant, but when she came on the line she told Kacy she already knew who she was. Her mom had been at the police station by 7:00 the night she was supposed to come home at 6:00. Her family and the people at the lab had convinced the police something had happened to her, even though they had to wait a while to see if she would turn up. Bethany and Sonya had gone to the station, too, to be questioned. Kacy could just picture the commotion in her mind. Wow — the three of them would have a lot to talk about. She knew she should be concentrating on the sergeant's questions, but she couldn't help thinking ahead to when all of this was over. If it ever *was* over. She knew she wouldn't be safe until she was in a police car going home. Her legs and arms were beginning to hurt from being so cramped up.

"KACY!"

"Yes, sir? I mean yes, ma'am?"

"Listen to me very carefully. You seem to be fading out here, and we can't have that. We're going to figure out where you are so we can come and get you. Give me the phone number on the phone you're using."

"But I want to talk to my mama." Yikes. She hadn't called her mom "Mama" in years — she thought it was too babyish. Where did that come from? And why was she crying all of a sudden?

"Kacy, listen to me, honey. You'll talk to your mama very, very soon. You've had a hard time, but you'll have to hang in there for a minute. Can you do that for me?" The voice was nice.

"Yes."

"Kacy, look around you. The computers are slow today, and while we're trying to match the phone number to a location, I'll see if you and I can figure out where you are."

"I can't look around me. I'll have to stand up in the booth and they might drive by here and see me."

"I want you to get up on your knees, or stoop just enough so your eyes can see out the glass of the booth. You don't have to stand up all the way. Tell me what's across the street or down the street from you."

"Well, there's a big plant of some kind right across the street."

"Good. That's great. Is it one building? Is it more than one story?"

"No, it's a whole bunch of buildings. It looks like a power plant to me. It has all those electrical things sticking up around it."

"Maybe you're near a Texas Utilities station. Can you see any signs?"

"No. . .Yes, wait a minute — there's some kind of sign on the gate, but I can hardly read it. It says 'Norton

76

Sub-Station' — at least I think that's what it says. There are stores down the block. Don't ask me to go to them. I'm too scared they'll come back in the dirty green car they picked me up in."

"You're not going anywhere. I'm sending out a police call to search across the street from the Norton branch. They'll be there in two minutes. We have cars cruising all over the place, and one of them is close to the area. In a couple of minutes, look out and see if you see a marked police car driving by. If you do, get out of the phone booth and wave at it."

Kacy was excited now. She stayed on her knees, but raised her head to keep looking out the glass of the phone booth door.

"It's here! It's here!" Without waiting for an answer, she left the phone hanging by its cord and stepped out of the booth to wave.

The car pulled up and two policemen jumped out. They whisked her into the back seat of the car, and one of the policemen sat beside her. "You're safe now," he said. Kacy sank back in the seat, happy, but too tired to talk.

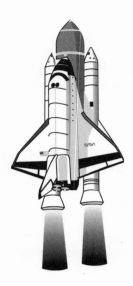

Chapter 15

The Police Station

THE REUNION AT THE police station was wonderful. Not only were Mom and Tom there, but Sonya and Bethany too. Mom burst into tears when she saw Kacy, and Kacy wanted to cry, too, but she was suddenly too happy to do anything but grin at everyone.

"I was still scared, even in the phone booth," she told Mom, "but now I feel safe at last."

Tom could only look at her with amazement. "I was plenty scared, too, Squirt," he said. "I was worried I wouldn't have you to push around anymore." He gave her a big bear hug and swung her off her feet.

"We made them bring us along, " Sonya told her as they all gathered in the lobby of the police station.

"Yeah," Bethany said, "I haven't been able to sleep for two nights, and when my mom called me at school to tell me you were home, I grabbed Sonya and we left school with only a note telling Ms. Harris where we had gone. We figured they'd *have* to understand, and if they didn't, we'd already be out of there."

Kacy could only shake her head and look at them with a silly smile on her face. She was so happy she had such great friends.

The police sergeant called Kacy into her office for a briefing on exactly what had happened. As soon as Kacy started doing some actual thinking instead of simply being glad she was home, she sat straight up in her chair and gasped.

"What's the matter, Kacy?" The sergeant seemed alarmed. Kacy's face had gone pale.

"Oh, no. What have I been thinking about? We don't have much time," Kacy said. She was so excited she almost yelled it. How could she have forgotten? She looked at the clock on the wall. The mission had already been in orbit for several hours. Rosie and the crew could be in terrible danger. She must talk to Mission Control.

Kacy had lots of experience in talking people into things, but these police people were the hardest yet. She was put through to another sergeant and a lieutenant but was unable to convince them that contact must be made with the space shuttle. After all, they had no real proof of what she was talking about, the officers told her, and it took a real emergency to break through on the airwaves to a mission already in orbit. They didn't want to interrupt the workings of NASA for something they weren't even certain about.

Kacy huddled with Sonya and Bethany, who had known about that weird Sam from the beginning.

"Why not call someone at the lab?" Sonya suggested. "They'll believe you."

"That's a great idea," Kacy said.

Andy sounded alarmed when Kacy called and told him about Sam. He promised to get through to someone higher up and call her back right away at the police station.

"I think we have at least a day," Kacy told him, "because I heard Sam say the poisonous chemical would begin to leak on Saturday. That's tomorrow. We don't have

79

much time to contact Rosie, and I'm afraid something will happen to her if she touches that poisonous dirt."

"You can count on me," Andy said. "I'll make them listen."

Kacy felt better after the call, but she had no time to make any plans. She was called back into the lieutenant's office for more questioning. As the questions kept coming, Kacy remembered more and more. She told the police that Sam and Donna would be returning to the warehouse in a few hours, after dark.

"That makes sense," the lieutenant said. "They might not want to show their faces until after dark. If they're headed out of the country, they'll probably try to fly out of here during the night or early tomorrow morning."

"What do you think Sam would have done with me, if I were still there?" Kacy asked.

The police officers just looked at one another. Finally, the lieutenant spoke. "They would probably have released you when the ship was safely in orbit, Kacy."

Kacy wasn't so sure. "But I saw their faces. I could identify them."

More silence. Then the sergeant said, "Well, there's no use dwelling on the past. We don't have to worry about that now."

Kacy knew, without their having to tell her, that the kidnappers could have tried to get rid of her for good. She was so thankful *that* was in the past. Something, though, kept nagging at her about Sam's return. She had no time to think about it, because just then, the phone rang in the police station. It was for the highest ranking police officer on duty that afternoon, who happened to be the lieutenant. He was to bring Kacy to NASA headquarters as soon as possible. The NASA flight director asked to speak to Kacy and he complimented her.

"We're very proud of you, Kacy, for being so brave and figuring out how to escape," he said.

"So you believe me?" she asked the flight director. "You believe what happened with Sam?"

80

"We certainly believe you're sincere. We just need to ask you lots of questions."

Kacy knew what that meant. Because she was a kid, they'd have to go over her story again and again before they really believed she didn't just have an active imagination. She was excited about the prospect of visiting Mission Control, but she dreaded all that questioning.

Kacy hated leaving Sonya and Bethany, who had been the biggest help of all. Not only had they suggested calling the lab crew for help in talking to NASA, but Kacy knew she could count on them to always believe her. Although they weren't allowed to go to Mission Control with her, she felt she might need them to verify her story about Sam. Before hanging up with the flight director, Kacy asked him for his private phone number — a place where she could be reached without having to go through all the departments at NASA. He gave it to her, and they said goodbye.

Mom and Tom insisted on going with her. Mom said she wasn't ready to be separated from her little girl at all that day. "Maybe I'll keep you with me forever," she laughed, and Kacy didn't question her. She wanted Mom and Tom along too.

Before she left the station, Kacy suddenly remembered what had been nagging at her. She had an idea, and she asked Bethany and Sonya to go to the restroom with her. The three of them huddled around the sink in the small room.

"Look, girls, I'm worried about something. I want you to do me a favor — like old times."

"So what is it?" Bethany asked. "You'd better hurry before someone comes in here."

"I know the police are planning to be at the warehouse after dark. But I'm worried that Sam might come back before then. He didn't like Cheryl being so friendly with me. What if he wants to check up on her, and comes back early to surprise her?"

"You heard what the police said about them being

81

afraid to show their faces in daylight," Sonya said. "What are you worried about?"

"I don't know. I'm just worried. Can't you go do some spying for me? You can still be home by supper-time if you leave now, and I need you to hide yourselves in that phone booth and call me if you see the dirty green car."

"But we've never seen it," Sonya said.

"Yeah, but she's told us what Sam and Donna look like, and we know it's an old rusty green car with the paint falling off. How many old cars like that will be passing by with two people in them? I know we can tell it's them," Bethany said. "I think she's right."

"And I can't be in two places at once," Kacy told them. "I can't be at NASA and in the phone booth too. You can be my eyes and ears. Get a taxi and go to the Norton Substation Power Plant and have the driver drop you directly across the street next to the shopping strip. You can't miss the phone booth there because it's the only one. How much money do you have?"

Bethany had two dollars and Sonya had three — she had just gotten her allowance.

"Wait right here." Kacy left them and took Tom aside. "I need some money to give Sonya and Bethany. How much do you have? Don't ask me why. You just have to trust me."

"You're lucky you just got kidnapped, Squirt, because I might not be in such a good mood otherwise. I have twenty-one bucks, and I don't think I've ever given you that kind of money before."

"*Lent* me that kind of money, not given it to me. Let me have all of it."

Tom handed the money over. "I take it you'll fill me in later?"

"You bet."

She had the world's best brother — at least for now. Kacy ran into the restroom and handed the money to Bethany, along with the private phone number where she could be reached at the flight director's desk.

"I'm off to NASA. Wish me luck," she said.

"Wish *us* luck," Sonya whispered.

"Don't forget to take quarters," Kacy mumbled over her shoulder.

Bethany gave her a look. "We're not stupid, Kacy. And remember — this taking orders stuff is going to end when this is all over. You're just going to be plain Kacy then."

Kacy didn't look back, but she couldn't help smiling to herself. If they only knew how much she did wish all of this would be over.

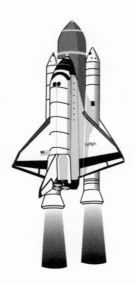

Chapter 16

Plans Overboard

THE TRIP TO NASA was fast. As Kacy explained more about Rosie and the crew to the police lieutenant, he became as impatient as she was, and he ordered the driver to put on the siren for part of the trip down the Gulf Freeway. Kacy had to admit that, as nervous as she was, it was really exciting to be in a police car with the siren running. They roared into the NASA entrance and were directed at once to the building housing Mission Control, the lifeline to Rosie's space shuttle.

When Kacy walked into the Flight Control Room she had to blink her eyes a couple of times. *Wow!* A bunch of people were sitting around watching about twenty television sets. She looked more closely and saw that the screens were really computer monitors. On a far wall was a huge projected monitor that everyone could see. The person sitting at each of the smaller screens had a big looseleaf notebook to work with, and each place was marked with a sign — "CAPCOM," "FD," "FDO" — all representing controllers who were helping Rosie's shuttle crew perform their activities in space. They watched every movement made by the crew and spacecraft, and made up the support center for shuttle communications.

The police lieutenant signaled to one of the controllers watching the big screen, and a tall man left the computer area and came out to meet them, bringing another man with him.

"I'm the flight director you spoke to before, and this is my payload officer," he said. "I understand there's a problem."

The lieutenant seemed embarrassed. "Look," he said, "I know you're in the middle of an important flight here, and we shouldn't be taking up your time. I can't even explain the problem to you. This young lady here has a rather fantastic story to tell, and maybe I'd better let her tell it."

Kacy was amazed that the flight director himself had come out to see her. She was a bit shy herself to take time away from someone so important to Rosie's work. But she forged ahead. This was no time to hesitate.

"Sir, I'm Kacy. I guess Andy and Joan in the lab told you about Sam, the custodian."

"Yes, and they told me about your space experiment too."

Kacy started her story about Sam and the poisonous chemicals one more time, and both men listened without a word. When she was finished, the payload officer spoke.

"Kacy, our problem is that we're hesitant to interrupt a mission when we don't have Sam here to question. The lab workers said you were very reliable, but you're only a child, and these are important decisions."

"If I could just talk to Rosie," Kacy said.

"I don't think you should count on that," the flight director said. "We'll relay any information. But are you sure you heard Sam say the poison was set to go off the next day out?"

"Yes, and that's why I was afraid to wait until they captured Sam and Donna and Cheryl. If we don't get them until tonight, it might be too late for the astronauts to do anything about the poison."

"You figured right," the flight director said. He sighed and turned his back to them, looking toward the big computer room. He stayed like that for a while, and Kacy kept quiet.

"Stick around, Kacy," he finally said. "I've decided to get Rosie on the voice communications system. Why don't you come in to my desk and sit beside me?"

Kacy couldn't believe her ears. She had no words to say — she just followed the director through the doors and into the glass-enclosed Mission Control Center. She sat beside him at his desk, marked "FD." He even had a Diet Coke can on his desk, just like he was doing something ordinary instead of getting ready to talk to someone in orbit. He put on a headset containing earphones and a microphone which reached around his chin to his mouth. Before Kacy knew it, she heard him talking to Rosie!

He told her Kacy was fine and he didn't say much about the kidnapping, Kacy noticed. This was probably because he didn't want to upset her while she was in orbit. They talked for a while, and Kacy took the time to look around the room at all the other controllers watching computer screens with rows of numbers scrolling up and down. She could just imagine all the scientific information flowing to keep the orbiter in flight.

The director turned her way. "Kacy, Rosie would like to speak to you."

"What?" She couldn't believe it. "To me? From space?"

"Go right ahead and talk."

"What do I say?" Then Kacy heard Rosie's voice.

"Hi, Kacy! How's the weather down there?"

"Rosie!" Kacy found herself saying things she hadn't wanted to say. "I'm worried about you. I'm afraid the poison stuff will ruin your crystal experiment."

"What did Sam say, Kacy?"

"He said the poison would start leaking a day out — that would be tomorrow — but maybe he meant one minute after midnight tomorrow. I don't think you have much time."

The director took over the phone, and Kacy didn't have a chance to say a proper goodbye. When he hung up, he turned to talk to her.

"I'm sending Rosie a data copy of everything you've told us, Kacy. But I think she's already decided to go into mid-deck and carefully remove your plant from the rest. It will be sealed, and when the other astronauts perform their extravehicular satellite repair, we're going to take the unusual precaution of releasing the daisy into space so there's no chance of Sam's plan working. We usually bring everything back to Earth with us, but it's fortunate that plans have been made on this flight for activity outside the orbiter. While we're out there, we can let it go into space. I'm sorry I couldn't let you talk longer, but there are too many decisions to be made, and talk is something we ration here."

"I don't mind. I just want the mission to be safe. I wish my daisy could have stayed with the other experiments, though." Kacy was trying to be brave about this, for Rosie's sake.

"Here's a message for you from Rosie. Want me to print it out?"

"You mean she typed me a message from space?"

"Yep. Here it is."

Dear Kacy,

I'M SORRY YOU HAD A BAD TIME. I'M SAD, TOO, THAT YOUR WONDERFUL DAISY WILL HAVE TO BE PLACED OVERBOARD. BUT I WANT YOU TO REMEMBER SOMETHING. YOUR PROMPT ACTION MAY HAVE SAVED OUR WHOLE MISSION HERE, AND YOU WERE VERY BRAVE TO COME BACK AND WARN EVERYONE. ANOTHER THING YOU MIGHT WANT TO THINK ABOUT: NOW YOUR LITTLE DAISY WILL ORBIT THE EARTH AND GLOW IN THE HEAVENS, LIKE A STAR.

LOVE FROM ALL OF US UP HERE,
YOUR FRIEND, ROSIE

"I never thought about it that way," Kacy said to the

director, "that my daisy could become like a star. That's even better than having it come back to Earth."

"I agree," the director said. "How many people get to have something of their own in orbit? We're very proud of you, Kacy. Rosie has complete faith in you, and we have based a big decision on your word."

"Do you believe me too? Even though I'm only a kid?"

"I certainly do. Our next step, now that we know that the crew is getting rid of the poison, is to get those creeps who kidnapped you. The police are going to take you along tonight, to be at the scene in case they need iden- tification when the kidnappers come back."

Kacy could hardly absorb any more news. Being at the scene was more than she could ever ask for. Well, not more. She did think of one more thing she wanted. "Can I take my message from Rosie home with me?"

"You can't take it home today, but I'll carefully save it and send it to you. Right now we must keep everything as confidential as possible until we know the project is safe. You've been more help than you know, Kacy."

What a day. Kacy couldn't believe anything more could happen, but it did. One of the phones on the flight director's desk, the one marked "Private," began to ring. The director picked it up and gave it to Kacy.

"There's an urgent phone call for you, Kacy. I can hardly hear, but it's from someone named Bethany. She sounds as though she's in a noisy phone booth."

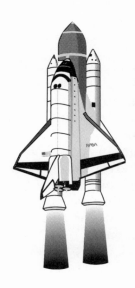

Chapter 17

The Dangerous Round-up

BETHANY WAS BREATHLESS, and Kacy couldn't make out what she was saying.

"Slow down, Bethy, I can't understand you."

"I'm trying to talk while I'm leaning down," Bethany said. "I don't want them to see us. We took a taxi and told the driver to take us to the power plant. We just saw the dirty green car you talked about, and it just started circling around the block of the place you told us to watch — that empty looking building with the two wide doors at the front."

"I can't believe it," Kacy said. "They *did* come back early. They must be driving around to make sure no police cars are around. Stay down so they won't see you."

"We are staying down — we're so scared we're practically on top of each other. After this phone call, I don't think we'll be able to leave the booth until they're inside and can't see us."

"Can you stay on the phone for a few minutes? Hold on. The police lieutenant might want to talk to you."

Kacy turned around. She'd been too busy with the phone call to notice that everyone was looking at her.

The lieutenant stepped forward. He had been listening to Kacy's end of the conversation, and had already called someone on his portable phone.

"The NASA people won't be in on this part," he said, "except for one of the lab workers, Andy, who will help us identify Sam, the custodian. I've got units headed to the area near the Norton plant. Good thing we pinpointed the warehouse on our map before we left the station. I'm amazed they would try to come back early."

"Well, remember that they think I'm still there and that nothing is wrong," Kacy said. "They're also being pretty careful to case out the block."

"'Case out the block'? Sounds as though you've been watching a lot of detective shows on TV."

"My mom doesn't let me watch a lot of the really violent shows, but I read that in a mystery." She handed the phone to the lieutenant. "You'd better speak to my friends yourself," she said. "I don't know what else to tell them, and I know they'll feel safer talking to the police. Their names are Bethany and Sonya."

"Bethany? Sonya?" The lieutenant spoke quickly. "You've helped the police more than you know by calling and warning us while Kacy had to be here at Mission Control. I want you to stay down, inside the phone booth. Just try to relax and wait. We know you're there, and after our police cars come there in a few minutes and go into the warehouse, we'll be coming for you. Don't go to the police cars. Just let them do their jobs and we'll find you afterwards. We'd also appreciate it if you'd not make any phone calls until we get there."

The lieutenant hung up the phone and said that the girls had agreed to stay put. Kacy felt relieved, but wondered what would happen next.

"How will we get there quickly enough?"

"How would you like to ride in a police helicopter, Kacy?"

"You've got to be kidding! Of course I'd like to!"

"The helicopter seems to be the way to go. If the kidnappers drive around for maybe another five minutes, we still want to keep our cars back until they go into the warehouse and we can get them in the same room where they kept you. Our units on the ground will do the dangerous work, and I'll only be flying you and Andy back there for identification, so we'll know we've captured the right people. We need to wait until the police cars get to the scene first. We wouldn't want to roar in and show our hand too early."

Kacy and the lieutenant said goodbye to the flight director and his staff.

"We're grateful to you, Kacy," the flight director said. "Rosie is hoping to photograph the soil of your daisy before she lets it go into space. Maybe the poison will be housed in some sort of visible container."

At that moment, Andy came into Mission Control. Kacy ran to him and hugged him. "I'm so glad you're going with us," she said.

"Me, too, Kacy. You've had quite a time of it, haven't you? We were really worried when your mom called and said you hadn't shown up at home after your session at the lab."

"You can talk later," the lieutenant called out. "Right now, we're ready to roll."

Kacy and Andy were taken to the rooftop of a nearby building, to a heliport set up for the landing of the police helicopter. The heliport was no more than a big space marked off on the flat roof for the helicopter to land. Kacy heard the roar of the copter first, and before she knew it, the shiny unit had landed right on target, blowing wind as hard as a hurricane from the Gulf. The engine kept running, and she realized the pilot was not going to shut it down. She, Andy, and the police had barely jumped into the shuddering helicopter when it lifted off.

The whirring blades were so loud that conversation was impossible. Since Kacy always had plenty of ques-

*Kacy looked out the window and saw three people
being led into separate cars.*

tions, she could hardly stand not asking them, but she knew she would have to wait. Strapped into a seat by the window, she had never felt so excited.

The helicopter followed the highway up to a point, then turned and headed over the treetops into one of the neighborhoods near Clear Lake. Kacy was a bit dizzy from the turns, but she was too excited to care. The pilot and the lieutenant were busy talking over the headphones.

"Come in, come in." Kacy could hear a lot of static as the police cars from the ground tried to make themselves heard. All she could really hear was squawky talk, but the lieutenant kept her posted.

"The green car has already been parked," he yelled, "and two people, a man and a woman, have gone into the warehouse. Our patrol cars are surrounding the place, and have all the exits blocked. They're on their way in, and there's no reason we should wait now. We'll pick a place to land and be on the ground in minutes."

Kacy had some questions, but the lieutenant shushed her. She was used to that, and figured she'd better shut up for a while. She certainly didn't want to be responsible for anything going wrong now.

As they landed in the middle of a parking lot on the side of the warehouse, the lieutenant told Andy and Kacy to stay seated in the helicopter, in their seat belts. They would not be getting out, but would just look out the window. One of Kacy's questions had been whether such a short flight was all they would have, and now she realized she would be flown back to the police heliport.

"Can we get Bethany and Sonya now? I'm worried about them," she yelled as soon as they had landed. "Can they ride back with us?"

The lieutenant shushed her again. Kacy looked out the window and saw three people being led into separate cars. "That's Sam!" Kacy shouted. The lieutenant looked over at Andy, and he nodded. Sam had on his same oily looking brown coat, and he kept his head down as he was thrust into the back seat of the police car.

"And there's Donna and Cheryl!" Donna kept her head down, too, and hunched over, while Cheryl kept looking around at all the cars, as if she were totally surprised and confused. Kacy remembered that she might still be dopey from the pills.

Kacy could hardly stand it. She felt safe now that they were all in police cars. After three police cars had pulled off for the station, another patrol car drove right up to the helicopter door.

"I think these girls deserve a ride back," the uniformed driver said to the lieutenant.

Sonya and Bethany jumped out of the car and climbed into the helicopter. They were beaming.

"We did it, Kace!" Bethany said. "And you're safe and sound."

The three of them squeezed into two of the back seats, and Andy and the lieutenant crawled out, saying they would make the trip back in a car. That left only the police pilot, copilot, and Kacy, Bethany and Sonya, who couldn't stop hugging each other and grinning.

They gave their secret handshake — each one gripped the elbow of one of the others, in a circle. With their fingers, they tapped out their secret code on the point of the elbow next to them. They forgot all about the handshake, though, when the propeller blades started whirring in a shriek, and they found themselves lifted straight off the ground over the buildings and trees.

"Isn't it great?" Kacy shouted. "I kept wishing you were with me."

Even Sonya, who got carsick a lot, looked out the windows and forgot about being even the tiniest bit afraid.

The three of them were flying high.

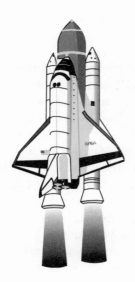

Chapter 18

Surprise

IT HAD BEEN THREE days since the kidnapping, and Kacy was dressing for what she knew would be the best school day of the year — even better than the day Rosie came to visit her science class. She couldn't find her favorite lucky red heart socks from Valentine's Day, so she decided to get dressed barefooted and hope the socks turned up at the last minute. She could hardly believe so much had happened.

When she had first returned home, she slept in her clean, warm, wonderful bed for twenty-four hours. Mom let her miss a day of school, and told her when she awoke that Tom had looked into her room every few hours, just to check on her. He would never have told her that himself. For breakfast she got to have two bagels with cream cheese, a glass of chocolate milk, and a peach. Mom told her she'd been very brave, and that her dad would have been proud of her, but that she'd gone crazy with worry while Kacy was away and would never want to repeat those days in a zillion years.

Then came a whole round of appointments: one with the doctor to make sure she was OK, another with the police to get a statement, and still another with the NASA people to confirm all that she had heard about the criminals' plans.

Sam, Donna, and Cheryl had confessed to putting the poison into Kacy's plant and kidnapping her so the poison could go into space and damage the mission. They had been hired by industrial spies working for a rival corporation beginning to grow its own crystals, and were paid to make sure NASA scientists would not produce protein crystals in space. If the crystal experiment were ruined, the medical uses for those protein crystals would be delayed for years, and the rival company's crystals would be the only pure ones available. Rosie reported from space that the crystals were now growing perfectly, just as planned.

As glad as she was that the criminals were captured, Kacy hoped they'd go easy on Cheryl, since she was the nicest. She was going to write a letter to the court telling them about Cheryl. Kacy would have felt much more scared if Cheryl hadn't been there. All the spies swore they would not have harmed Kacy, but she wasn't so sure. Sam and Donna seemed mean enough to do anything, and Kacy shuddered, thinking how awful it would have been if she had not been able to escape.

Kacy looked in one last place for her Valentine heart socks and found them — under the bed. She felt doubly lucky now, and was relieved she wouldn't be late for school. Of all days, this was one she didn't want to miss. Mom even offered to give her a ride to school, something she almost never did since she had to be at work early.

Kacy should have suspected something was up when Mom parked the car instead of just letting her out, but she was so eager to see her friends that she jumped out of the car and ran up the school steps. As she came into the wide entrance hall, she saw a big banner stretched above her. It read: "WELCOME BACK, KACY!"

Ms. Lackland's music class was there with a drum, two trumpets, and a keyboard, playing band music. Best of all, everyone in school was standing in a wide circle to greet her. They had all arranged to be there a few minutes early for the surprise. Even Tom was there. He was standing by Mom, who had sneaked in behind Kacy.

"You're speechless for a change, aren't you?" Ms. Harris came up and put her arm around her. "You certainly gave us a scare, but we were all thinking of you the whole time you were gone."

"I've never been so surprised in my life," Kacy told her. "Especially at school."

Principal Traynor was standing with Ms. Harris, and he reached out to shake Kacy's hand. "We're very proud of you," he said.

The first bell for classes had just rung, and Mr. Traynor asked the students to adjourn to the auditorium. He led Kacy to the stage with him.

"I want to give you a special medal of excellence, for being so brave and helping NASA protect its mission in space. We're so glad you escaped unharmed and that the kidnappers have been caught. And we also want to call to the stage two people who were very important in bringing the criminals to justice."

Kacy was thrilled when Sonya and Bethany were called up to share the applause. They all three hugged.

"Did you ever think this would happen?" Kacy whispered to her friends.

"Not with the three of us, I didn't," Sonya said. "Just a while ago you were thinking of yourself as an outcast, Kacy. A lot can happen in a few months."

"Well, if I was an outcast, you two kept me from going completely nuts," Kacy whispered.

Kacy had just begun to think nothing more exciting could possibly happen when the auditorium doors opened and the television crew from Channel 2 came in, led by Carly Prince, Kacy's favorite anchorperson.

"Sorry we're late," Carly said to Mr. Traynor. "We

had to cover a big fire on the other side of town. We want to get some footage of your Girl of Honor here," she said.

"I don't have to make a speech, do I?" Kacy asked.

"Absolutely not," Carly said. "We'd just like to have your principal give you the medal again."

"I'll do better than that," Mr. Traynor said. "An official of NASA has just come to join us."

The NASA representative shook hands with all of them, and said, "I want to give you this scale model of the space shuttle *Discovery,* Kacy, and bring you greetings from the astronauts in space, especially your friend, Rosie Ruiz. She's looking forward to meeting with you when she arrives back on Earth."

Kacy, Bethany, and Sonya managed a few thank-yous for the camera. Mostly, the three of them were huddling together, deciding whose house they were going to meet at tonight to watch the evening news.

"You're an awfully good team," Carly said to the girls. "Something tells me this isn't the last adventure you three are going to spring on us."

The three of them looked at each other and laughed, but before they had a chance to think about what Carly had predicted, someone tapped on Kacy's shoulder.

She almost fainted. There, beside her, stood her science teacher, Mr. Wall. At least, she thought it was Mr. Wall. He loomed above her in his usual way. He wore the same black and brown heavy tweed jacket, with the same brown leather patches on the elbows. But something about him was very, very different. He looked younger, and somehow neater. It took her a couple of minutes at least to realize what had changed. Then it hit her.

Mr. Wall had shaved his beard.

"A deal is a deal," he said.

Later that night, when the evening news was over and her friends had gone home, Kacy walked out to the edge of the woods behind her house. It was very dark. A recent rainfall had cleared the air so that the few stars out were almost within touching distance. The blackness had a fragrance to it — damp and sweet.

Kacy looked over the treetops, and thought of the time her butterfly wings had taken her soaring not so long ago. It seemed years had passed since that day. She thought of all the times she had almost given up on herself. Keeping going wasn't as easy as it was cracked up to be.

One particularly small star flickered in and out among the leaves of the tallest tree around. The star appeared and disappeared. Just as it seemed to go away, it was there again. Nothing could stop it.

Kacy knew that all the nights of her life the star would be there in her mind's eye.

"That's it," she told herself. "That's my daisy."

Glossary of Astronaut ABC's: Space Terms to Remember

astronaut   A person trained to pilot, navigate, or otherwise take part in the flight of a spacecraft.

atmosphere   The gaseous mass surrounding Earth and kept in place by the Earth's gravity.

countdown   The counting backward aloud from a starting number to indicate the time remaining before an event, such as the launching of a missile or space vehicle.

Discovery   One of the space shuttle orbiters in the shuttle fleet, named after two exploration sea vessels — one sailed by Henry Hudson and the other by James Cook.

external fuel tank   This tank holds liquid hydrogen and liquid oxygen propellants for the three main engines found in the winged orbiter's tail.

extravehicular activity (EVA)   Activity or maneuvers performed by an astronaut outside a spacecraft in space.

flight director   Leader of the flight control team, responsible for the overall shuttle mission, payload operations, and all decisions regarding safe, successful flight conduct.

hatch   An opening, as in the deck of a ship or in an aircraft.

liftoff   The instant at which a rocket or other craft begins flight.

mid-deck   The living, eating, and sleeping area for off-duty crew members, as well as a research lab where many experiments can be conducted. It is located below the flight deck.

Mission Control Center   The control center where all manned space flights are controlled after liftoff.

mission specialist   Mission specialist astronauts work with the commander and the pilot and coordinate shuttle functions for crew activity, consumables usage, and payload operations.

orbit   The path of a celestial body like Earth or an artificial satellite as it revolves around another body.

pallet   A portable platform used for storing or moving cargo or freight.

payload   The passengers, crew, instruments, or equipment carried by an aircraft, a spacecraft, or a rocket, or the income-producing part of a cargo.

payload officer   Coordinates onboard and ground systems between the flight control team and the payload user, and monitors the Spacelab.

robot   A mechanical device that sometimes resembles a human being and can perform complicated tasks on command or by being programmed.

solid booster rockets   These rockets straddle the external tank and provide most of the thrust for the space shuttle's launch to space. Two minutes after liftoff they are returned to the ocean by parachute for later reuse.

space shuttle   A reusable spacecraft with wings for controlled descent in the atmosphere, first designed to transport astronauts between Earth and an orbiting space station and to send out and retrieve satellites.

Spacelab   A complete scientific laboratory carried by the space shuttle and designed for zero-gravity operation.

Suggested Reading:
From Jules Verne to Sally Ride

Beasant, Pam. *1000 Facts About Space.* New York: Kingfisher Books, 1992.

Becklake, Sue. *Space: Stars, Planets and Spacecraft.* New York: Dorling Kindersley, 1991.

Chartrand, Mark R. *Planets: A Guide to the Solar System.* New York: Golden Press, 1990.

Docekal, Eileen M. *Sky Detective: Investigating the Mysteries of Space.* New York: Sterling Publishing Co., 1993.

Embury, Barbara. *The Dream is Alive.* New York: Harper & Row, 1990.

Hansen, Rosanna, and Robert A. Bell. *My First Book of Space.* New York: Simon & Schuster, Inc., 1985.

Mayes, Susan. *What's Out in Space?* Tulsa, OK: EDC Publishing, 1993.

Moore, Patrick. *Space Travel for the Beginner.* New York: Cambridge University Press, 1992.

Ride, Sally. *To Space and Back.* New York: Beech Tree Books, 1991.

Rogers, Mary Beth, Sherry Smith, and Janelle D. Scott. *We Can Fly.* Austin, TX: Ellen C. Temple & Texas Foundation for Women's Resources Publishers, 1983.

Verne, Jules. *From the Earth to the Moon . . . and a Trip Around It.* New York: Scribner, Armstrong & Co., 1874.

About the Author

SHARON KAHN's adventures as an arbitrator, attorney, and free-lance writer led her from the North Pole to space shuttle manufacturing plants in Texas. A pioneer in electronic reporting since 1985, she writes weekly news articles and book reviews under her byline for Compuserve's *Online Today*. Her special interest in children's literature culminated in a bachelor's degree with honors in English literature and child development at Vassar College, a master's degree in English literature, and a certificate in early childhood education. In 1992 she was a top ten finalist in the Pacific Northwest Writer's Conference Literary Awards for adult short story. She lives and writes in Austin, Texas. The mother of three, she now enjoys reading to her granddaughters, Emma and Camille.

Sharon Kahn presents writing workshops for children featuring Your Own Writer's Kit — Everything You Need to Begin Your Career as an Author.